To A

I love you,
Keep being strong,
you can do it!

))

Heaven Help Us

Someone save our souls

By Kitty Mae Atkins

♭

For all who are going
through mental health
problems; stay strong and
keep ploughing through.
You can do this, I believe
in you.

For my family, who have
kept me strong with love
and care.

And for Alex, my Donnie.

Chapter One

Upon my evening arrival at the Mental Hospital, there were two things of which I was immediately certain;

One: I was officially a Mental patient.

Two: I had not packed nearly enough underwear.

A few months ago I didn't think I would end up in here. A psychiatric unit that is. I'm not a child of a misunderstood nature and a haunting past. My best friend at age eleven, made me do particular things to her, whilst she

did the same to me. As a
child I didn't have many
friends and was bullied
from age six, then age 10
through to the end of
secondary school, by
various different people.
I developed insomnia at
age fourteen and anorexia
at fifteen. Depression at
ten and hallucinations and
alternative personas of
myself at age sixteen,
when I was admitted into a
mental ward, after an
overdose that landed me in
hospital a few months
before. I have suffered
from self-harm from age
eleven, after my so-called
best friend introduced me
into self-harm as well as
bulimia. Nevertheless,
here I was, and despite my

past I would try my
hardest to focus on a
future of some sort. Or to
learn how to live in the
moment.

My beginning few hours at
the inpatient consisted of
waiting, swallowing
sleeping pills and being
perpetually scared
shitless. Though I would
not leave my room, a
gaggle of girls entered
the doorway to my cave and
introduced themselves.
Inhaling gusts of wind
into my heavy lungs, I
prepared myself to walk
out of the entrance to the
outside hallway, in which
the radio squawked
repetitively, and girls

hummed and squealed like
talented piglets.

Slipping my fingers into
the door handle, I flung
the block of wood aside,
and swam into the open.
The first thing I noticed
was the scars scattered up
and down the arms of
patients- thick and thin
red blotches that hid
secret stories and
unpleasant memories.
Despite my efforts, I
could not help but stare
in awe at this freedom not
acceptable in society, yet
blessed and to the norm in
here.

Stumbling later that
evening into my room, I
fell into bed, and as I

gulped the small blue
sleeping pill down my
throat, I finally slipped
into a somewhat
comfortable sleep.

~

Eyes snapping open like a
nervous Venus flytrap, I
awoke to the rhythmic
beating of nurses knocking
on doors. I launched
myself out of bed and was
dressed and ready before
knuckles could be placed
on the precious panel
betwixt the hallway and I;
the hallway which I was
inevitably to go down. The
day slithered mockingly by
like a snake stalking its
prey; I was told I must
finish my toast and my

bathroom door was bolted
in case I were to purge-
regardless of my history
being clean of forceful
vomiting, despite my past
attempts. A sports day was
held in the garden, where
I willingly passed on
participation and rather
watched, drowning in
knitwear and blankets
thrown over me due to my
complaints of the cold.
Afterwards, I was told to
review my 'story' with a
nurse, which was followed
in the evening with my
very own consultant. He
mixed up my facts with my
other facts which stapled
confusion in the equation.
However, he suggested
medication which I was to

begin on the following day
or two.

One patient was to be
discharged the next day,
so a party- generic but
morbidly entertaining- was
thrown. Far too much food
lounged on tables,
emitting a tasty, pungent
aroma, in which I
regrettably gave in to
once or twice. Meal times
appear to be my least
favourite thing about this
place. My genuine refusal
and slow nibbling has
already frustrated staff,
so I was threatened with a
meal plan on several
occasions. A young girl in
the ward follows a meal
plan, though I see how
much pain and grief it

overwhelms her with. She
shakes and quietly sobs at
the dinner table, and I
empathise with her genuine
fear of the calories
dropping into her stomach.
This girl is as young as
thirteen, and goes by the
name of Jasmine.

As soon as I got past the
hyperventilation's and
anxiety attacks nestled in
my head, I plucked up
enough courage to talk to
her. Once, she was crying
and I rested my arm around
her for support, instead
of using words, though I
was told not to interact
with her as "Jasmine needs
to do this on her own."

~

I sulked out of the
dreaded kitchen, and as I
was on my way to my room,
I squeezed a plastic cup
filled with water between
my fingertips nervously.
As I walked past, a small
voice squeaked from the
sofa behind me, and I
heard my name,

"Would you like to play
Monopoly with me?"

Spinning around, I was
caught off guard, and my
speech faltered. Human
interaction? My heart
palpitated- I hesitated.

"Uh...sure."

I followed the young girl
into a communal room,
where she began to set up

13

the board. Paper rustled
as she shifted dyed money
into piles. Launching my
share at me, she made
casual small talk, "so how
did you get in here?"

Drowning in a hail storm
of rainbow coloured money,
I choked on my words,
picking them carefully out
of the air as I was with
the bills,

"oh you know, the usual
lot," she looked at me
steadily, hazel eyes
bearing into my skin. I
gulped,

"Self harm, suicide,
hallucinations, anxiety,
eating disorders..." she
nodded and shuffled her
winnings,

"what about you?" I
questioned precariously,
"if you don't mind-"

"Uh, originally- self
harm, suicide, uh," she
breathed heavily, but
tried to hide it,
"hallucinations,
anxiety..." her voice
trailed off and I nodded
softly, uttering a
sensitive response.

Later that evening, I
perched on the sofa with a
few patients. One had
long, sweeping, light
blonde hair, and wore a
loose fitted purple shirt.
Another had dark, brunette
hair- long and hanging
past her shoulders- went
by the name of Kate, and

was someone I found
incredibly attractive.
Lastly, a petite black
haired girl- Kenya-who
arrived a few weeks ago.

The radio is kept on a
constant repeat, which is
frustrating due to the
amount of times particular
songs seem to appear. As
we were talking, a certain
song began to play,
containing the word
drowning in the lyrics.

"Why can't Natasha listen
to this song?" A voice
asked from next to me
about the girl I had just
played Monopoly with, and
we all waited in
expectation for a
response.

16

"She was in an accident."
Purple shirt casually
replied after a short
pause. She motioned to her
chest and stomach area and
waved her hands,

"She was drowning, and she
almost died."

A chill slithered down my
back. I felt everyone's
head slowly nod. Soon
after, I was sat next to
Kate. She bobbed her head
towards my arms, after I
had anxiously slipped off
my cardigan,

"Your arms look like
they're fading."

"Yeah," I flashed my eyes
to the neat, red lines

17

crocheted across my skin,
"I guess they are."

"You haven't self harmed
since you've been here?"

I half smiled and ducked
my head. Twirling the hard
skin around my
fingernails, I opened my
mouth to reply,

"Well-"

"Yeah." Kate smiled. Her
lips smoothed into a grin
with ease, brightening her
wonderful face. Background
noise intensified until I
realised I was being
spoken to,

"Have you ever had sex?"
The petite black haired
girl gawked at me from the

opposite sofa, and I
shuffled in my seat.
Uncomfortable, I replied,

"No, I've never actually
been in a relationship-" I
was interrupted by a
subtle chorus of awe's.

"Have you?" I was
interrupted by a subtle
chorus of yes's. The black
haired girl spoke again,
"are you straight?"

"*Kenya*." someone hissed. I
thought carefully about my
reply. I went for a shrug;
easiest option,

"I don't know."

Laughter.

Another brunette- taller,
and wearing skin tight
jeans- had finished her
phone call and sat next to
Kenya for a while, but
was now about to leave for
bed. As soon as she got
up, Kenya turned and posed
a question,

"have you ever had sex
El?"

"yeah," she said matter-
of-factly, and the girls
continued their
conversation, but El
muttered something under
her breath- discretely,
but still loud enough for
me to notice her
unfortunate habit,

"one by choice, one
against my will."

20

Her murmur sent a chill
throughout my entire
nervous system. A silent
scream that sent alarms
sending the harsh reality
down into the core of my
bones.

El was a rape victim.

As she stalked away, Kenya
threw herself on the seat
next to me. Sweeping her
hair into a neat bunch at
the side, she let the
curls hang over her
shoulder, tumbling in a
dark cascade.

"How long are you gonna be
here?"

"I don't know," I
stuttered, "how long have
you been here?"

"a week," she stated
profoundly, "but they said
I'd only be here two
weeks."

"that's good,"

"yeah," She looked me in
the eyes, and giggled- a
stiff kind of laughter, it
wasn't fake, but not true
either, "but they're never
really honest."

"why are you here? If you
don't-"

I shook my head and
waggled my palm at her-
second time lucky,

"self harm, suicide..."

Refusing to go in to
detail and being over-

dramatic, I cringed and
half-heartedly laughed,
"what about you?"

"I tried to kill myself."
She announced it almost
too casually, like she's
rehearsed it a hundred
times before, and waited
her whole life to tell it
this way. My eyes
automatically flickered to
her wrists, and I saw they
were clear. *Don't ask how,
that would be rude.* We
vaguely discussed the time
we both spent in hospital
after our major attempts,
until she sprung off the
coach to do something
else. I listened to the
topic of conversations,
not eavesdropping cruelly,
just listening out of

interest, and the topic
seemed to be boyfriends.
Kate lounged in the empty
space next to me and I
avoided eye contact,
though she swivelled to
face me. Her eyes shone a
light green, and her
eyelashes traced them,
long and thick with
mascara. She spoke, hushed
and cheekily, like it was
a secret she had been told
to never speak of,

"I have a girlfriend," she
laughed softly, ringing
like wind chimes in my
ears, and a grin was
spread evenly across her
face, forming her pale
rose lips into a curve. I
accidentally mirrored her
smile,

24

"do you?" it wasn't a
question, more of an
automatic response. She
nodded, and I smiled
timidly- almost everyone
here is in a relationship.

Chapter Two

Today wasn't such a great day, and it aggravated me that no one cared. The dimly lit night sky viciously burst through spaces in the window, forcing ice cold air into my room, causing me to coil a blanket over my body. Inked to the brim with scars, I glanced down at my flesh. They were more noticeable now too. I stood in front of the warped plastic mirror, and scowled at the girl standing opposite me. Red lines trickled across my skin from my calves all the way up to my shoulders. My thighs, stomach, ribs, chest, arms

- all merely a destruction
site.

My body is a canvas, and
it has been ripped to
shreds in anger and
sadness.

From nature we were
moulded out of clay and
shaped into perfection,
but as a work of art I do
not feel even slightly
adequate, not even enough
for a cheap painting sold
at an auction. Rather, I
feel like a three year
olds interpretation of
Picasso's blue period. I
feel like the meaningless
block of squares some
artists paint. I feel like
that smudge on the wall
that you cannot get rid

of, and no matter how hard
you try to scrub it, with
all your might, it is
never coming off. You are
burdened with this black
smudge; you don't know how
it came to be, or who put
it there, but it is what
it is, and it's derisory,
useless and irritating.

I am the black smudge.

Growing rapidly confused
at my metaphor, I curled
up on my bed and thought.
A black smudge. A black
smudge lives its life
pasted against a
moderately clean wall, and
is one day mercilessly
slaughtered by strong
polish. Yet, the black
smudge holds a better life

than me; though we both
sit on the sidelines and
gaze at the word spinning
in fast motion, as we are
plastered on the wall, the
black smudge can escape.
The black smudge can
decide to become invisible
and just disappear,
without a care or another
germy say in the world.
Slowly, I have become the
black smudge, learning its
ways and practising its
methods. Though when I
decide it is my time to
vanish, it becomes a large
deal when the act doesn't
go to plan.

Plunging my earphones into
my ears, I forced my eyes
shut, feeling the rhythmic
pulses of notes floating

through my head. Dinner
came and I was surprised I
did not start sobbing.
Being told I had to eat
"or else" contributed to
my overly pessimistic view
of the day so far. I met
my family on the way back
to the ward, and as we
went upstairs, we passed
the other adolescent
patients. Kate looked at
me, and spoke. Two words
slipped out of her mouth
that significantly altered
my mood, something so
simple; it made me want to
rip my heart out and give
it to her, "well done."

~

Knelt in a homemade semi-
circle, I sat with a group

of patients and we spoke.
They say you learn
something new every day,
and despite my negativity,
my pessimism proved to be
false during our
conversation. Natasha
explained how she could
see some things
constantly, "a butterfly
and a frog," she expanded,
nodding slightly, "and
someone named Joe." Her
mention of this anonymous
Joe sparked my sympathy
antennae's. One girl,
Ella, had scratches on her
hands and straight pink
hair, falling corpse-like
above her collarbones. She
briefly described her
characters, mentioning how
she could see a woman and
a young boy. The boy was

ok, she had previously
announced, but the
woman..."

"...tells me to do bad
things."

We silently shuddered,
imagining the harsh
severity of imaginary
friends. Ella motioned her
head towards a door to a
bedroom; around three
metres away from the
corridor the five of us
were situated. A cold gust
of air shuffled through my
skeleton, sliding through
my ghost like structure
with ease. We waited for
Ella to speak. She spoke
in a hushed tone, with a
hint of disguised shame.

"He's here now."

Balanced like an angel and
a devil on her shoulder
were her two friends and I
respected her illness. But
it also scared me, to
imagine seeing the voices
I could hear, springing to
life. Another girl leant
against the wall with her
knees tucked in to her
chin, wearing a shirt with
'Soul' printed across the
blue fabric. Soul
explained how she has
anorexia, and that as a
young child, she was
sexually abused. The
amount of people who were
raped in here disgusts me
to the brink of vomit and
hurts my heart.

Kenya was someone I had
taken an instant liking

to, due to her
hyperactivity and honesty.
During the conversation, I
accidently bumped the
topic to me, and I
explained my anorexia.

"Purposeful?" Kate was
positioned on the floor,
legs flailing in the air.
I shook my head,

"Bless your heart,"
muttered Soul. I will miss
these patients. I didn't
think I would, but a
friendship-less life of
mine was being transformed
and I'll actually miss
them.

Chapter Three

"I don't want to go in my
room."

I clutched my knees with
entwined fingers. My head
subconsciously shook, and
I saw blue strands of hair
trickle in front of my
face.

"oh honey," Kate muttered.
Half-smiling, I choked
back tears and rested my
chin on my bones,

"do you wan' a cuddle?"

I nodded, and slid off the
table onto the carpet. I

faced Kate cross-legged
and she reached for my
palms. I heard my name
ring in my ears and a
staff member sulked
towards me,

"call for you."

Kate released her light
grip, and I lethargically
sauntered towards the
telephone,

"hello?"

"hello." The voice dripped
into the phone and I
smiled goofily.

"hi."

"how are you?"

"I don't want to go in my room Donnie."

A short pause felt like a year,

"why?" I sighed deeply and took in a sharp intake of breath,

"in case I hurt myself."

"oh..." he whined painfully, and I felt bad. Donnie didn't need my incessant moaning right now.

~

Crouched on the ground, Soul walked past, "you ok?"

"Not really," I breathed, peeling my hands from my face.

"You want to talk about it?" I shrugged, then looked up. Her face looked kind; honest. Dragging myself up, we collapsed to the ground outside of Soul's room.

"What's up?"

I quietly studied her face. Symmetrically beautiful; her fragile bones framed her small head. Her eyes were bright and framed by perfect brows; Hazel all over, with porcelain skin. Yes-I was overwhelmed with jealousy. I drastically sighed deeply,

"everything." I dragged
the blue across my
forehead, and threw back
my ratty locks in rapid
motion. Balancing my feet
on the wall, I felt her
eyes glance at the red,
laddered on my arms,

"How long have you been
self harming?"

"Since I was eleven,"

"Wow," she whispered
breathily, "you've done
well to stay out of here
for that long,"

"Yeah," I muttered. We
stood outside her door and
she coiled her arms around
me. I felt her breath
pattern as her shoulder
blades pressed into my

palms. As we let go, she
quietly uttered,

"Stay safe." My brain
perked up and I felt tears
oddly well up in my eyes.
I gulped, "you too."

Chapter Four

I wafted into my room,
breathing in every last
drop of the home-scented
aroma, speckled around
like dust particles
dancing in the light.

I missed home.

I fished around my back
pack and threw in a new
tube of moisturiser,

"Oh yeah, I need to take
this back-"

I paused suddenly. My
brain whirred and clicked
like intricate clockwork,
and I spun around to look
at my sister, who stood
silhouetted by the window.
Her small frame was
engulfed by sunlight, and
an aura shone around her
skin like an extended
soul.

I swallowed a hard lump
emerging in my throat,
"know what I was about to
say?" she shook her head,
golden hair flinging
graciously around her
neck, "no, what?"

"I was gonna say 'home'"

"But it's not your home,"
her eyes glistened with
worry,

"I know I just…" I turned
back to the bag, blue
licking my cheek, and
frantically packed,

"Slip of the tongue."

~

As I stepped into the
adolescent ward hallway,
the corridor of my second
home had a pungent aroma
of stale fish. Patients
were slouched on sofas,
and my name was chorused
lightly as I entered. The
welcome knocked me out of
my bad mood bought on by
dinner back at home.
Lounged on the sofa, I
contemplated, Two days
weekend leave was not
enough, but next week I'll
get to sleep at home *if I*

don't do anything stupid before then.

I slotted a film into the TV and threw myself on the couch next to Kate. Curling into a ball, I clutched a pillow, burrowing my fingertips into its soft exterior and breathing softly into it. In the midst of the chosen flick, the door creaked open slightly. The six of us simultaneously focused our attention on the silhouette in the door way. Milly slipped through the door and leant on the wall, with a pure expression of innocence and sadness. Diana spoke first,

"Y'alright Milly?" Milly
nodded, unsurely, and
another voice I couldn't
match to a face in the
dark chipped in,

"You wanna watch?" She
shook her head.

Silence filled the room
with an echo-like essence.
I sucked in a mouthful of
crisp, hospital air and
scrunched my nose in
distaste. I looked up at
the blonde, curling locks
falling in a waterfall
piled on top of Milly's
skull. I cleared my
throat,

"Would you like a hug?"
Milly shook her head and I
sighed quietly. She
stalked over to Diana,

where they whispered to
each other for a while. I
felt Kate's eyes on me,

"D'you want a hug?" I
shrugged,

"It's all I'm good for," I
laughed faintly and Kate
shuffled in her seat as I
squeezed my pillow,

"Aw," She cooed, and
giggled quickly, "I'll hug
you,"

I swivelled my feet to the
ground and Kate leant
back, resting her head on
the pillow curled in my
lap. I arched my arm
around her and laid my
forearm along the side of
her back, and we stayed
like this throughout the

duration of the film. I've
never hugged anyone like
this before, and I must
say it felt incredible.
Kate emitted a scent of
flowers and girl, and her
hair was long and soft,
wrapping around my fingers
as I twisted strands in my
palms. It took me a while
to realise that stroking
her hair behind her ear
would be unnecessary,
despite however tempting
it was.

The film ended and Kate
sat up, smiling sleepily
at me before walking out
of the room. I sighed
breathlessly, and dropped
my shoulders, *what was
that?* I mentally shouted
at myself for over

thinking it; *it was just a hug for Christ's sake dude*. El was sitting on the couch opposite, and she stumbled over to the place in which Kate was just sitting, flinging cards in front of me as she turned to face me, looking me straight in the eyes like a mirror. I looked down at the cards and back up at El, with a look of utter confusion on my face. Her lips turned upwards and she burst into a fit of laughter, in which I quickly picked up, as I shuffled my share of cards and we began to play a card game.

I flickered my eyes to the clock. It wavered and

pulsated as I tried to
tell the time, and I
realised it was past
eleven. We stopped
laughing and I staggered
up from the couch. Tidying
away the cards scattered
on the floor, I trotted
over to the tall brunette,

"Night El," I hugged her,
and she squeezed back.

"Goodnight."

Chapter Five

Toes gripped the base of my shoes, and I clutched my heart. My lungs ached and squeezed and I closed my eyes. I halted, and breath escaped me like a rush of prison escapees – reckless and fast. Hyperventilating, I called for the staff member walking in front of me, with two other patients. Quietly screeching her name, tears dripped off my chin silently and I was told to focus on my

breathing. I was sat down
on a public bench and
Diana gripped my shaking
hand. Too many people was
the cause of my panic
attack, and as if on cue,
once I had slightly
recovered, there was a
significantly reduced
amount of people clustered
in the town. "So proud of
you," Diana whispered in
my ear, and I kept
listening to my breathing,
hand clasped over my
heaving chest. My first
trip to the town did not
go as well as I had
planned. Trailing behind I
stabbed my fingers into
the plastic bag, my
purchases hitting my thigh
with each shaky step.
Stepping into the taxi, I

perched in between the two
girls, clasping the
seatbelt nervously. By the
time we reached the
hospital, I had just about
regained my breathing, and
collapsed on the sofa once
we entered the adolescent
ward.

~

"You're not allowed to
watch this, it's
unsuitable for the ward,"
I moaned, imitating a
staff member, as we snuck
into the lounge to watch
the not-so-horror film.
Curled on the floor next
to Kate and Soul, a few
squeals occurred during
pathetic moments, claimed
to be scary by the other

girls. Fifteen minute
checks came about more
frequently when you're
busy, or hiding something.

"*Who's in the mental
hospital?*" A character in
the film jokingly
questioned, and I
shuddered. I felt a shiver
rush through everyone else
in the room too. I sniffed
to fill the silence, "Me!"
Soul squawked, and we
giggled half-heartedly.
Wrapping arms around my
waist, I felt suddenly
more uncomfortable. The
door flew open,
interrupting a climax
moment in the film, "is
this the film you were
told not to watch?"

"It's CSI: Miami," Soul
called to the staff
member, shadowed in the
doorway.

"Like a box set?"

Fooling a staff member was
easy, but when a murder
took place on the screen,
it was far less easy to
cover it as an
entertaining crime show.

"Hey, yeah, this doesn't
look like CSI, can I see
the box?" We hesitated,
and I handed the DVD case.
A review claiming it to be
*the most terrifying film
of the year* didn't help
much.

Confiscated.

~

"I had a panic attack
again," I spoke into the
phone, fingers curled
around the landline wire,

"Oh no, that's not good…"

"I know." Donnie breathed
down the phone and I leant
against the heated
plastic, subtly warming my
cheek.

"Guess what?"

"What?"

"Today, it's officially
been a month that we've
known each other."

Expecting bad news, my
face lit up,

"It's our month-iversary,"
He chuckled and I smiled.
A month since I had
received a message on a
social networking site. A
month, and he's the best
thing that's ever happened
to me. I realised how
pathetic I was being, and
mentally cursed at myself,

"It's also been a week
since I came here." I
significantly lowered the
tone, and mentally cursed
myself again.

"I'll talk to you at the weekend though yeah?"

"Yeah."

"I love you."

"I love you too," I pushed the phone down on the receiver, and awkwardly walked over to Diana and Bella, who were standing near the hallway sofas. "Was that a boy?" Bella called, and I accidentally blushed,

"Yeah," that was a useless attempt to act casual.

"GET IN THERE," Bella cawed and I laughed, swinging open the door to my room.

~

I stood in the doorway,
shadowed by the dull,
fluorescent lights echoing
around me. I cleared my
throat and squinted at the
TV light glowing in the
near pitch black room.
With a shaking hand, I
smiled, and tapped softly
on the door. I poked my
head around the doorway
and saw a small girl
situated in her bed. I
said I'd say hello to the
new admission, but she was
now startled and gawking
at the strange girl shaded
in the entrance of her
room with wide eyes. I
gulped and maintained my
smile, despite her ill-
mannered response, "Hello,

I'm a patient here," I
paused, expecting a
response but to no avail.
I told her my name; still
no response. I sighed,
"Well, it's nice to meet
you." Nodding and grinning
like a maniac, I stepped
out of the doorway and
welcomed the tidal wave of
light washing immediately
over me. I gripped the
diary nestled in my arms
and attempted to slow down
my heart; clutching
something for comfort and
shut eyes did the trick
after a while. I told
myself never to do that
again, human interaction
is not one of your strong
points you *silly girl*. I
ambled over to the pool
table, where the girls

were still huddled. "So?
What happened?"

My eyes slid to the side
as I remembered what I saw
in the room. Darkness
mainly, and a bed, a
television, some towels,
and a girl. Lounged under
her duvet I could just
make out her appearance;
pale mocha skin and a
hurricane of light brown
hair, tumbling over her
shoulders and swept
carelessly into a sideways
ponytail. Samantha's face
consisted of large wood
coloured eyes and full
lips. I didn't have a
first impression, because
Sam didn't say anything;
perhaps just shy.

Chapter Six

You pathetic snivelling fool, where will all this whining get you. You're ugly and disgusting and you always will be. Maybe you should just end this now and get it over and done with, because no one wants you here.

Heads bowed and shivering bodies, we grasped on to each other's hands like we

were the only five left on
the planet. Everyone else
had vanished, earthquakes
ploughed into the earth
and tornadoes spat out
bodies. Blood filled
rivers like a human
milkshake, and bodies were
stacked like a pile-up on
the motorway. The ocean
shone black with pollution
and debris, and the sky
was no longer blue.
Nothing survived, everyone
and everything was
slaughtered mercilessly.
The only things that were
left, all that remained,
were us. Sat on the
carpet, we refused to let
go, we were a chain
interlinked with each
other. We knew that if we
were to let go, something

bad would happen. A staff
member was close to tears,

"Why won't you tell me
what's going on, talk to
me, please, I can help
you" babbling frantically.
My eyes were closed but I
spoke to the rapid voice
behind me,

"Bad vibes."

We all felt it; bad vibes.
And that's all it was, but
it felt to much more than
that. So much more. Ella
leant against my shoulder
and was sobbing
desperately, gasping and
spluttering in a fit of
tears. Gripping onto my
other hand, El had tears
dripping down her face
too. Holding on to Ella

were two more girls who were also crying. I sat in the middle and stared aimlessly into the distance, I was the glue. People rushed around in a daze; they came and left-blurs of light spinning around as I sat utterly Jaded. By the end of the night, only El, Ella and I were perched on the sofa-which we moved to sometime during the rush. I snapped out of my oblivious state and realised I was still holding their hands. I heard something mutter from across the room and I looked up at the clock; a white face grinned back out of my blurred vision, baring its teeth made up of numbers. A six and a

nine doubled as its fangs
and the clock hands
reformed to make slits as
its eyes. It cackled
cruelly and spat a number
on the floor in front of
my feet; its tongue
slithered back into its
jagged mouth, and its grin
transformed into a frown.
The number one appeared
from its mouth as a tongue
and flickered across like
it was licking its lips. I
blinked harshly, but it
was still there when I
opened my eyes. *Go away,
go away, go away.* I tried
to take control of my mind
but I knew it couldn't be
possible, the voices
continued to whisper and
bellow in my brain. I
glared at the smug looking

clock, mockingly laughing
as I stared at its ghastly
face. Voices in my head
began to argue with each
other, so my entire
conscience was filled with
screaming, shouting, and
laughing from the evil
timepiece. I glared at the
beaming clock; an
inanimate form of the
Cheshire cat, spitting
numbers which littered the
floor in front of me with
each time it opened its
sharp mouth. *You and Me
Clock,* I mentally spat.
Its eyes bent to form a V;
a child's interpretation
of a bird, and its numeric
jaws clamped shut. Voices
were drowned out by my
heavy breathing and
everything sounded as

though I was underwater.
Muffled silence thundered
in my ears, and banging
increased on the door to
the ward. Creaking
overwhelmed, and water
flushed through the door,
forcing a thick blanket of
blue over the entire
hallway, rushing into
everyone's rooms and
compelling me to release
my hold on the two girls
next to me; whom I
realised where frozen into
two large blocks of ice. I
wriggled my hand free of
the icy prison and they
floated of with the waves
into the distance, stuck
in the same positions.
Soon enough, the entire
ward was an underwater

city, but I could still breathe.

Water stabbed at my eyes and prodded at my ears, and as my gaze swum through the sinking numbers swirling in the water like they were being sucked down a drain, I locked my sight on the clock. Narrowing my eyes, I realised I was not sitting on the sofa anymore; I was hovering above it. I looked down at my feet and began to flip them back and forth, and whilst moving my arms in a breast stroke pattern, I graciously slid through the blue towards the clock. The sofas, tables and chairs were still in

the same position, but the
lid to the fish tank had
burst open, and fish were
twirling free in the
ocean, spinning softly
around my neck and body. I
suppressed a laugh and
focused on the clock,
whose own laugh still
echoed around the water. I
looked at the wall but the
clock was not there; a
hook hung mockingly in its
place and the number two
was pinned to it, like a
sacrifice. I gulped and
flipped around. The clock
flew towards me briskly,
zooming through the ocean
face first; the chilling
grin being the only thing
I could see. I hurried to
move out of the way but I
could not move. I looked

down at my body and
writhed but I could not
break free from invisible
chains. I tried to scream
but my breath collapsed on
me, and water crammed into
my lungs. I choked and
gripped my throat as the
clock flew towards me,
tumbling through the murky
water, growing closer and
closer to my face. I
squeezed my eyes shut,
suffocating, I felt my
heart falter. With a final
cough my eyes fluttered
open and my vision
collapsed, only seeing the
top of the water moving
further and further away
as I sank to the ground; a
dark abyss. My heart came
to a halt and I slid into
the black hole, not

choking or screaming, just
an overwhelming pain in my
lungs as my vision faded
to black. The last I heard
was the laughter from the
clock. Cackling, no,
giggling in my ears.
Giggling…

My eyes snapped open and I
gasped for breath,
smothered by the air
swimming into my lungs. I
slowly became aware of my
surroundings; the fish
were in the fish tank, and
I was still holding El and
Ella's hand. The two girls
where the source of the
giggling, and the clock
was plastered on the wall-
no daunting face or scary
grin, just jumbled numbers
and horrid hands. The

numbers where placed in a
circle and the hands where
positioned on the twelve
and the two. I looked down
at my feet, the number had
gone, and my feet were
placed firmly on the
ground. I flung my head
back and sighed. Bad vibes
indeed, I needed to go to
bed.

Chapter Seven

It was late evening, about
ten o clock, and I was sat
in the hallway outside of
Kenya's room. Darkness
engulfed us, except for a
lamp plugged in the socket
near where we sat. I had
just come back from a
weekend at home, but had
quickly changed into my
pyjamas after my parents
had left. I had been told

that usually the first
weekend at home was the
worst, but in reality, it
wasn't all that bad. I was
kept busy so I didn't have
too much time to think;
Friday was a day out,
Saturday was a day in, and
Sunday we went to the
cinema and then I was
taken back to my second
home. That's when it had
gotten bad. Playing happy
families was fine but
after the cinema,
depression swept over me;
a tornado of sadness. That
afternoon I had made a
plan, and once I had
subconsciously changed and
sat down with a group of
patients, I was almost one
hundred percent certain
that there would be one

less person at the table
in the morning. Before I
sat in the car on the way
back here, I made a
decision. Donnie was a
very important figure in
my life, but sometimes,
things were hard. Perhaps
that's a bit of an
understatement, Donnie was
going through similar
things to me, and all I
wanted to do was make him
happy. Unfortunately, some
things he said were
triggering, and I also
couldn't handle being
locked away in 'recovery'
while he was struggling
alone. I was in selfish
oblivion, and all I could
think about doing was
ending my life. So I said
goodbye. The word appeared

on the screen in front of
me and I pushed the
letters coinciding with
the awful farewell.

I flicked open my eyes and
saw Natasha reach out for
my hand- I was back in the
hallway outside Kenya's
room. My heart was
palpitating viciously and
I wasn't sure what was
happening, it was blind
panic mixed with guilt
mixed with *what have I
done* and *I want to die,*
and the attack struck me
hard with a knife,
stabbing me multiple times
in the chest in which I
recoiled at each harsh
wound. I gripped onto
Natasha's hand,

"Um, I-"swallowing hard, everyone stopped talking. I choked on the silence and my eyes went to the staff member sitting on a chair about a metre away, just staring at me and the commotion,

"I-I can't breathe," I screamed, and started hyperventilating. Natasha and Ella came closer to me and spoke in a loud but soft voice, telling me to breathe and calm down. A chorus of voices called for staff and I saw eyes locked on me. I shut off from everything and lost control. My hands shook vigorously and I felt palms stroking my back.

"Look at me. Come on, look at me."

I looked helplessly into Natasha's eyes and tears managed to slip carelessly down my face. After a while, the girls had managed to calm me down and I was slowly breathing again. The staff finally came and the man sitting on the chair got up and left. Complaints about how shitty the night staff were rung around me like incoming telephone calls, loud and assertive. A few patients went to bed while staff members helped me stand up and walk shakily to my room. One lady came into my room and attempted to give me a 'one to one'

conference, but obviously,
I was not in the best
state for a therapy
session. When I came back
outside, three patients
were left sitting on the
sofa, and I plunged on the
seat next to Ella,
clasping my hands around
my knees now pulled up to
my chin. Sometimes you
just want to be around
people, and not on your
own. I knew what would
happen if I went into my
room, and I wouldn't have
any control over it
either. Staff kept calling
for us to go to bed for it
was too late, but Ella
explained,

"We don't feel safe in our
rooms," the rest of us

nodded and I buried my
head in my knees. An hour
or two passed and everyone
had gone to their rooms;
probably not sleeping
though, for lights
extended on the ground in
a rectangle outside
various rooms. I had taken
sleeping meds however, and
was drifting into a numb
and dull sleep. A staff
member wedged open the
door to my room as I
rolled into bed, dragging
the covers over me and
willing myself to sleep.
My heart thumped
unsteadily and my breath
abated as I floated into
obscurity.

Chapter Eight

I woke up startled. *I'm alive.* I couldn't decide on what my emotion was; relief, disappointment, sadness? I felt the light spilling through the window frame like a warm embrace and I shut my eyes, feeling the sun pressing against my eyelids. Soft knocks on the door came and went and

I crumbled to the floor
out of bed, clothes
sticking to me like a
magnet as I stumbled past
my wardrobe and slipped
out the door. After
breakfast I was in a
constant state of
numbness. I curled up into
bed complaining of feeling
unwell and slept through
lunch to the afternoon.

I woke up startled. *Am I
alive?* Monotonous light
forced itself dully
through the window
opposite. With an enormous
amount of effort, I
lethargically pulled
myself up and sat upright.
I curled my head and
stretched my arms,
unknotting knots tied in

my spine with a satisfying
crack. As I rolled my neck
I noticed a piece of paper
on the chair next to my
bed. Reaching for the note
I underestimated the
distance and collapsed to
the ground in a crumbled
heap. *Ouch.* I moaned and
rubbed my knee, eyes still
half shut. I squinted in
painful realisation of the
throbbing headache I
remembered I had. I rolled
around and snatched the
piece of paper from the
chair, sitting cross
legged on the carpeted
floor and leant my head
against the cold bar of
the hospital bed. My eyes
skimmed the note and I had
to read it a few times

before processing what was
written,

Dear _____,

*I don't know you that well,
but you've helped Jasmine so
much. I wanted you to know
that I love you,*

*Stay strong, you can get
through this bullshit.*

Love Soul

A smile expanded across my
face as I continued to re-
read the note. How
beautifully random of a
patient, I didn't know
Soul that well but I have
had conversations, and
knew her well enough to

know that she seemed nice, despite her issues. I scampered over to the bedside table, and fished around for a packet of blue tack. Ripping a ball of tack from the paper, I pushed down four blobs in the corners of the note, and fastened it underneath the various posters attached to my wall. Standing back, I put my hands on my waist and admired the note. Head cocked to the side I heard a rustling outside my door, followed by a soft tap. As a staff member waltzed in I quickly glanced at the clock by the side of my bed. Three O clock? *I've slept nearly the whole day*. I turned my head slightly and said a sleepy hello to the woman in my doorway. She reminded me about a community meeting, in which the whole ward meet to discuss any issues one may have, and I uttered that I'd be there soon. I dragged my sheets over the bed in some sort of order, and took one last look at the note before pulling a hoodie out of my wardrobe and tugging it on. I stood in front of the mirror and took it all in; bags under my eyes, pale blotchy skin and messy hair tangled maladroitly into a clip at the back of my head. I sighed. *I guess this is as good as it's going to get.*

Community meeting finished
faster than expected, as
there was generally
nothing much to discuss.
As I made my way back to
my room, a staff member
muttered my name,

"Someone for you on the
phone."

I gulped. I really didn't
think Donnie would call, I
honestly thought he would
never want to speak to me
again, and just abandon me
like everyone else. Of
course that wasn't what I
wanted, so why did I keep
fucking things up so much.
I coughed and picked up
the phone off the
receiver. I sat on the
chair and it occurred to

me that I was shaking- a
lot. Stuttering, I took in
a deep breath and closed
my eyes, waiting to hear
his voice,

"Hello?" I tried to sound
confident, but my words
spluttered like a failing
car.

"Hi."

A sea of emotions washed
over me. Guilt mostly,
nervousness, happiness- it
was like I was about to
start a conversation with
a stranger. It had only
been a night, but I felt
like everything had ended
and we were to start anew.
I remembered I was on the
phone and the pause felt
deafening,

"I'm sorry-"I began, but
he cut me off with rigid
laughter,

"-for starters," I
continued, swallowing back
pure embarrassment, "I
didn't think you'd call
so, thanks…"

"Oh I had to," He said
matter-of-factly, "I had
to make sure you were ok."

I smiled drearily.

"How much of what you said
did you mean?"

Suddenly, I remembered
everything I said and my
heart fluttered. *Shit.* In
my defence, I didn't think
I would make it to the
morning, so my

ridiculously cheesy and embarrassing messages where necessary in my point of view. Still, I *was* here, and he had read my messages, and I was considerably fucked. I took in a shaky breath and steadied my wavering hand, "I can't remember what I said; I wasn't all…there."

"Yeah, I could tell."

I wiped theoretical sweat off my forehead in relief, and after a while, the conversation had to come to an end. Flinging the phone back on the receiver, I strolled casually to a group session held a few doors down from my own, in the lounge. Still shivering, I was not entirely sure whether it was from my increased dosage of medication, or after my phone call with Donnie.

As the group came and went, dinner soon arrived to my dismay. Evening crawled past and consumed me whole as I made my way dozily to my room. Night time routines consisted of giving everyone a hug, and as I came to Soul, I whispered in her ear,

"Thank you for the note, it was really sweet,"

She looked at me and smiled, "that's ok,"

"I love you too, ok?"

Chapter Nine

Dress swaying tenderly
over my thighs, I zipped
up the back with caution,
avoiding the lace
crocheted on my shoulder
blades; fabric embracing
bones with its lacy
fingers. Perching on the
couch, I brushed imaginary
dust off my lap, and
dragged the material over

the plasters placed above
my knees. With a sigh, I
glanced at the other
girls, settled on the
sofas and hanging around
next to the arms-
clutching a stiletto or a
half empty packet of
biscuits each. I tilted my
head to my legs and felt
uncomfortable; milky skin
stretched over bones
smothered in fat, and
scars laced from under the
knee to the top of my
thighs. Thin and thick,
red and white, fresh, old,
nasty words etched into
skin- all regrets, and a
constant reminder of my
mistakes. The dress
allowed some recent cuts
to be visible, and people
kept pointing at the

plasters, so I quickly
changed into something
more suitable, despite the
'prom' that was to take
place. In all honesty, it
was poorly organised, and
after dinner, almost
everyone was back in their
nightwear.

The days before had been
terrible; malicious voices
and intimidating thoughts
intruded my mind. However,
after my long rest the
previous day, I felt much
better. Prom was a
colossal let down, though
not entirely. Rather, we
talked to each other and
watched movies, which in
my opinion is better than
a party any time.

Wednesday came and went;
an eagle skimming across
land to catch its desired
victim, swooping past
graciously but dangerously
in order to seize the
prey. A backwards day, I
awoke later than usual and
was tired almost the whole
day. The morning consisted
of painful writers block
and the longing to go
outside. The sun ruptured
through clouds and
produced licks of light
across the grass, seducing
the dew clinging to each
blade and motioning with
long fingers for me to go
and join them.

Sigh.

We watched two films in
the morning in celebration
of a lazy day; *Tangled* and
Pitch Perfect were not
entirely to my taste, but
were wonderful and
enjoyable none the less. I
curled up in the dark next
to Soul, who offered me
globules of chocolate
every now and then, in
which I politely accepted
to due to my tolerable
mood. Savouring the candy,
caramel danced across my
taste buds, sparking my
brain to make me feel
guilty and terrible about
eating. I ignored them-the
voices- brushed them away,
as I proudly swallowed the
remains, and half-
heartedly smiled to
myself.

That evening, we had finally decided where we were to go. Before dinner, Kenya, Bella, Soul and I followed a staff member to a park situated just down the road. The heat was overwhelming, and although Bella and Soul had scars laddered up and down their arms, I still did not feel comfortable having my arms out in the open just yet. We clambered up on a children's climbing frame and perched on the top next to the slide. I leant against a pole next to Bella and threw my head back, soaking up the sun and outside air, inhaling every last drop into my lungs as though the air would run out. The park

was near empty, and
serenity squeezed us with
silent arms. Soul was
talking to the staff
member just below us on
the climbing frame, and
Kenya sat opposite as I
turned my head to join the
conversation.

Walking back to our second
home, we arrived just in
time for my (insert
sarcasm tone here)
favourite time of the day-
dinner. With my shoulders
hunched and a disappointed
expression, I dragged my
chair away from the table
and threw myself down,
sitting sulkily in front
of the cheese sandwich.
Nibbling nervously, I knew
I had to finish it, or I

would not be allowed out
this evening. I finished
all four quarters, leaving
remnants of grated cheese
and flakes of brown bread
on the plate.

"Who was told they had to
have something else with
the sandwich at lunch?"

I averted my gaze from the
staff member in the
doorway and preyed she
wouldn't mention my name.
The room filled with
silence and she repeated
the question,

"*Who was it?*" She snarled,
and I continued to look
away. *Please no one say
anything, please-*

"Her," Milly nibbled her
sandwich and motioned
towards me, "it was her."

*Fuck you Milly you
uneducated shit.*

"Salad, yoghurt or crisps?
And you have to finish
that cheese," I glared at
the shavings of cheese on
my plate and laughed,

"I'm not having anything."

"You have to,"

"No."

"Then you can't go to the
cinema this evening."

I shook my head and sucked
back tears; I wouldn't

give her the pleasure of
my crying. I bit my lip,

"Salad."

A plate of salad was
thrown in front of me
consisting of coleslaw,
lettuce, cucumber,
tomatoes and potatoes. I
poked at the lettuce with
a fork, inspecting its
leafy like structure. *I'm
not a rabbit.* I was also
not eating that salad,
regardless of its lower
calories than the sandwich
I just had and the chips I
had for lunch- it was the
concept. I was full and
sick and I *had* eaten. I
did not want to eat any
more and that was that.
Bella cleared her throat,

"Can we go?"

"Not until she finishes her salad." I leant back in the chair and Milly glowered at me from a seat down from the staff member opposite,

"Eat it." She whispered, motioning harshly to the salad in front of me, and I shook my head. Minutes past and Kate looked at the clock,

"It's half past-"

"Can we *go* now?"

"Yes," the staff member mumbled, as chairs scraped quickly on the floor, and I scampered to get away from the table.

~

That evening was dreadful.
I untwined my fingers from
the telephone wire and
stared into the distance,
feelings rushing through
my head. I stalked into my
room and began pacing,
frantically gnawing the
skin around my
fingernails, looking for
somewhere- anywhere- to
go, but everything could
be used as a weapon and I
didn't feel safe. I
wandered into the bathroom
and smacked my head
against the wall, standing
momentarily with my face
against the cold. I turned
around and banged my
spine, gripping my face in
my hands as I slid down

the wall, falling in a heap on the bathroom floor, still wet from my earlier shower. I drew my knees up to my chin and concealed my head, sitting in an upright foetal position sideways against the bath. Blood trickled from the wound on my bicep I had made a few seconds before, and the plaster slipped off onto my lap, curling around its sticky self. A staff member called my name and I didn't respond, after a few repetitions I called back,

"I'm in here." I didn't turn to look at him but he stood in the doorway, and I felt his eyes on me,

"Come on, get up," I shook
my head,

"Don't disappoint me, get
up, please, come on…" this
carried on for a while,
before he left to get a
member of staff in a
higher position than
himself.

Fred crouched down by the
side of me but I kept my
head buried in my knees.
Why can't I cry? I felt
numb and broken and I
didn't know what to do or
say. Fred kept asking me
things and I responded by
moving my head,

"Do you want to self
harm?"

I nodded.

105

"Have you self harmed?"

I nodded again.

"Is it bad?"

I shook my head.

"How do you feel?"

I paused and then shook my
head again. Silence
engulfed us. I gulped,
"Empty."

"Say that again sorry?"

I cleared my throat and
said it louder this time,
quietly sobbing. My
shoulder shook up a and
down and I lifted my head
from my knees, still
avoiding eye contact with
the staff member crouched

beside me, as tears
finally slithered down my
face,

"*Empty.*"

"Empty."

I nodded. Fred sighed and
I tucked my hair behind my
ears. He spoke some more
and asked me to,

"Try and get up from the
bathroom floor."

"Ok."

He stood and stretched,
trailing out of the room.
I heard the soft thud of
the door to my room
closing and I launched my
fist into the bath. The
plastic rippled from the

force, and concaved
quickly before reforming
itself. I did it again,
but harder, squeezing my
eyes shut and tightening
my fist as it ploughed
into the harder rim of the
bath, and I cried out,
slamming my head against
it too as my fist recoiled
from the vigour.

I looked up at the ceiling
and whimpered, taking a
deep breath. I willed
myself to get up but I
couldn't, voices echoed in
my head and I felt
anaesthetized and wrecked.
I heard my breath
shuddering and I opened my
mouth, swallowing a hard
lump in my throat,

"*And we can run,*"

My voice wavered but I
continued to sing,

"*From the backdrop of
these gears and scalpels,*

*And every hour, goes the
tick tock bang of monitors
as*

*They stare us down, when
we met in the emergency
room,*

*And in our beds, I can
hear you breath with help
from cold machines…*"

I continued and completed
the song, and as I
finished the last word, I
hauled myself up. I wiped
my soaked face, cleaning

109

the black rivers of
eyeliner streaked down my
face like earthquakes,
before collapsing into bed
and sitting obliviously in
front of the television. I
staared at the moving
pictures on the screen and
basked in my state of
heedlessness.

And that was when I heard
it.

Chapter Ten

The scream ricocheted
around the entire ward,
causing doors to shudder
and beds to shake. Books
dropped off shelves and
wardrobes tipped face
down. Draws emptied and
collapsed to the ground,
spilling contents
everywhere, and windows
smashed, dispatching
millions of pieces of
glass around the room.
Perhaps that was slightly

over exaggerated, but
that's what it felt like;
a bloodcurdling sound that
ruptured eardrums and
disturbed sleep. I
clambered out of bed and
ignored my slippers,
kicking them aside as I
crept sleepily to the
door. Glancing at the
clock as I went past, I
squinted as my vision
adjusted to the dark; 1am.

Opening the door I slipped
into the hallway, shadowed
by the darkness
surrounding the hall, and
slinked towards the
commotion. Natasha stood
further down in the
hallway with a few staff
members surrounding her.
She stalked briskly past

them, waving them aside,
and a gust of wind flew
past as she brushed by me.
She ran into her room then
out again, pacing around
the hallway like a jaguar
in a cage. I walked over
to her and grabbed her
arms,

"Nat, Nat stop," she was
shaking, a lot, but she
wasn't crying; she looked
angry,

"Natasha listen, I've got
you, and it's going to be
ok-"

"No," she mumbled, and
shook her head,

"I've got you Natasha, I'm
here."

Chapter Eleven

"I am alive."

Clutching my heart, I closed my eyes. *Where am I?* My eyelids fluttered open and I spun around, gasping at my surroundings. Trees arched above my head, black and flaking, twisting around each other's trunks; branching out into a murky chasm. The moon was perched above the trees,

hidden amongst the
overgrowth, shining
sinisterly on the forest
floor. Looking down, I
realised I was barefoot;
feet buried under
deteriorated leaves.

Everything was black.

I stuck my hand out in
front of me, and twisted
it slowly as I admired its
dull colour. Pulling a
strand of hair in front of
my eyes, I noticed it was
no longer blue, just a
pale shade of grey, and I
threw it quickly back
behind my shoulder. Chimes
echoed in the distance,
and the trees creaked
solemnly, formed in a
circle around me. As I

115

turned around, the trees
seemed to spin too, and I
found myself feeling dizzy
and lightheaded. I
stumbled, and tripped over
a protruding root,
collapsing in a stack of
grey coloured leaves,
coughing and spluttering
in the dirt.

I looked up at the trees
in front of me, but there
was now something new. A
large mirror was hovering
in front of a coiled tree;
large and circular, smoke
revolved in its glassy
exterior. I rose slowly,
and stood in front of the
mirror, but could see no
reflection. I tilted my
head and stared into it.
Fog filled it like dry

ice, but there was no
smoke behind me. I moved
closer to the mirror,
stepping carefully on the
leaves, crunching as I
walked on their fragile
skeletons.

I was soon within touching
distance. Squinting at the
frame, I noticed the smoke
was spilling out of the
glass, forming a thick,
smoky blanket around my
ankles. I lifted my arm
and reached towards the
mirror, palms steady and
ploughing through the
smoke, the fog licking
around my fingers as my
hand grew closer and
closer to the glass. I
gulped and prepared to
stroke my finger on the

surface, but my finger
fell through, and I
reached into the mirror.

Further and further, my
hand began to disappear
into the smoke. I took a
deep breath, pulled up my
leg and stepped in. The
smoke smelt of bonfires,
but it felt cold. I was
standing in the mirror,
but my head was still
placed outside, one hand
perched on the outside
frame. I heard a cracking
noise and I twisting my
head but saw no one behind
me; trees embraced in
darkness mocked me. I
turned my head back to
face the mirror in front
of me, and a hand appeared
before my eyes; a smoky

hand with foggy tendrils.
It flew forward and I
screamed, and the hand
grabbed my face and
swallowed me in the fog as
I writhed and wriggled in
an attempt to free myself,
but to no avail. I was
dragged into the mirror
and I closed my eyes as I
was overwhelmed with haze.

~

I opened my eyes and my
vision hit me like a
straight out punch to the
face. I sat in the
classroom in front of the
computer, staring blindly
at the document open on my
screen. Voices
reverberated and I jumped
as I felt arms around me.

Yanking my headphones out
of my ears I turned to see
Natasha behind me, walking
over to the seat next to
me. I sighed in relief and
sat to face her. She
cleared her throat and
relaxed on the chair,

"Hey,"

I nodded in response, "Hey
there." She took my arms
and softly pulled up my
sleeve,

"I made this for you,"

"It's lovely," I said as I
glanced down at the
plaited thread she was
wrapping around my wrist,
and watched her as she
tied it in a secure knot,

"So whenever you go to
self harm, you see this
and think of me,"

She let go of the bracelet
and sat back, as though
she was admiring her
work," And then you don't
do it."

I smiled, "Thank you."

"Hopefully anyway, that
was the idea," she grinned
and I leant over to hug
her, coiling my arms
around her back, feeling
her breath against my
fingertips,

"Thank you," I repeated,
and let go as she nodded,
and then got up to walk
away,

I turned back to the
computer and shut my eyes.
Where did I go? I
remembered the haze of the
smoke caressing my face
and entire body.

Smacking my head in
bewilderment, I leant
against my palm and rubbed
my eyes, trying to pull
myself back to reality. I
opened my mouth and formed
silent words with my lips,

"I am alive."

Chapter Twelve

The scream chorused around the entire hospital. I rolled out of bed and sulked to my half open door. The staff had found me in the bathroom with cuts on my arms, curled in a ball in the middle of the floor, and they left the door open so that I wouldn't do it again. Although this procedure

was unnecessary, I was not
in the mood to argue.
Stepping timidly outside,
I looked around the
hallway. The lights
flickered on and the alarm
began to whir dauntingly.
I saw someone pacing.

"Wh-whats going on?" I
aimed my stuttering
sentence to the girl, and
she spoke without looking
at me,

"This is so fucked."

"Who was screaming?"

"El was." She walked over
to me and brought me into
a hug. Once we let go, I
noticed a red mark around
her neck. At the same
time, I noticed her

looking at my arms and
realised I was not wearing
a jumper.

"Oh-"She started and
pointed at my bloodied
arms. I waved her away and
half-smiled. A patient
yelled from behind,

"Soul, why did you press
the alarm-"

"Because everything is so
fucked," She spun around
and pointed to a recently
new admission, curled up
on the sofa. Her shoulders
shuddered in time with her
quiet sobs. Soul pointed
at the small framed girl,

"She's crying,"

She pointed at me, "she's
cut herself,"

Soul pointed at another
girl who just walked out
her room, "She's scared,
there are people trying to
kill themselves; *I'm*
trying to kill myself,"

"Soul-"

"El's crying, everything
is-"

"So fucked." I finished.

"Yeah."

"Emergency community
meeting," Ella shuffled
into the hallway and
proclaimed her
announcement. We filed
into the lounge and waited

in expectation. Kenya was
twisted on the sofa,
sobbing quietly, gripping
her fists tightly and
shaking her head.

"Kenya, Ken, give it to
me."

"Come on Kenya."

Kenya was shaking her head
frantically, as girls sat
next to her, asking for
the sharp object she was
gripping in her hand. It
was not working; Kenya was
getting more distressed
rather than anything else.
I dashed over to the sofa
and knelt in front of her
on the floor. I leant
forward and cupped her
face in my hand. In a
hushed voice I spoke to

her, as she reached out
and gripped my hand,

"Kenya, look at me." Her
eyes flickered to mine and
I moved closer,

"Ken. Everything is going
to be ok." She shook her
head and I nodded in
response,

"I'm here for you, I
promise," I held her hand
tighter, and rounded my
other hand over the one
she held the sharp object
in, "I'm not going
anywhere Ken, you're
safe."

Her hand squeezed
incredibly tight as I
slowly attempted to

wriggle my fingers in and
grab the blade,

"Come on Ken, it's me," I
forced my fingers in and
saw the point of the knife
blade gripped under white
knuckles, and blood
trickled steadily from her
shut palms,

"*Kenya*," I ripped the
knife from her grip and
she fell into my arms,
crying as I rubbed her
back,

"I'm so proud of you
honey,"

I leant my head on hers
and stayed in our embrace,
gripping the knife in my
hand and closing my eyes
in relief,

129

"So proud."

She sniffed and spoke
suddenly, "Help me."

I gulped and turned my
head, resting my forehead
on the side of her own
next to her ear. Kenya
smelt of forest fires,
cigarettes and an odd
scent of burning pansies.
She was warm, but
shuddered with each
hiccupping sob,

"Help me," she whispered
again, tears dribbling
down her cheeks and
collapsing on my hands
clasped around her own,
placed on her lap;
entwined fingers gripping
on for her dear life,

"*Help me,*"

"I will," I stroked her
hair and whispered softly
back into her ear, rocking
her back and forth like a
mother and her child,

"I'll help you, I
promise."

Chapter Thirteen

"I'm going to do something," I got up from the sofa and hit the pause button on guitar hero,

"Nothing bad?" Soul laid back on the opposite sofa, long blonde hair curling around the arm supporting her neck, and tumbling almost to the ground,

"No,"

"Promise?"

"I'm going to draw," I
replied, and remembered
the pencils in my room,
waiting expectantly on top
of my sketchbook,

"Not on your skin?"

I shuddered, and swallowed
a hard lump and my throat.
I laughed,

"No,"

"Okay," Soul smiled and
picked up the guitar I had
slung on the floor and I
began to walk out of the
lounge and down the
hallway into my room.

Throwing myself down on
the bed I switched on the

television and stared at the moving images. *Top Gear* slowly transformed into something else. I got up off the bed and walked towards the TV, standing blankly in front of it, attempting to figure out the blurred mixture of colours and swirling images contained in the box. The swirls began to drag themselves out of the television, and I wearily stepped back, blinking multiple times to try and get rid of the strange hallucination. The colours dripped out like a rainbow of wax, and slithered across the floor and around my feet. My feet were glued to the carpeted floor and I could no

longer move. Suddenly, I
heard a knock on the door
and the wax screamed-
running back and fixating
itself into the TV again.

I walked over to the door
and opened it to see
Purple shirt standing in
front of me. She handed me
a film,

"Watch it," she said,
looking me in the eyes and
holding the DVD in front
of me. I looked down and
took it from her. *Nothing
special.*

"OK, thanks." Smiling, I
gradually shut the door,
and spun around, hitting
my back hard against the
wood. I slid down and fell
onto the floor, sitting

with my legs apart and my
head on the side, leaning
against the door behind
me. *What the actual hell.*

I stepped into the hallway
and sat shakily on the
sofa. *Tonight will not be
a good night.* El and Ella
sat on the sofa opposite,
scared witless and
whispering carelessly to
each other. I kept my head
in my palms and attempted
to calm my shaking, though
my leg was relentless and
refused to halt. The
voices bellowed around me,
and shook the room,
shouting for me to look at
them, or else. I shut my
eyes tightly and thought
very hard, praying that

they would listen for
once,

*Look at you, what do you
mean?*

**Look at me you ignorant
fool.**

But I can't see you?

Yes you can.

The voice growled and I
slowly turned my head.

There it was.

Standing shadowed across
the room, towering over
everything and staring
hauntingly into my eyes,
he stood there watching
me. A tall, black
silhouette with no face,

just a tall black body,
and long wiry fingers and
claws. Next to him was a
smaller version of
himself, but completely
white.

I shut my eyes and tears
dripped down my face; I
was shaking vigorously and
I made small whining
noises every time I turned
to look at them. No matter
what, they wouldn't go
away, all they were doing
was standing there,
staring at me with empty
eyes and spooky
characteristics, telling
me to do terrible things
to myself otherwise they
would do it for me. I
began to sob hysterically
and the two girls rushed

over, stroking my palms
and telling me it would be
ok. *Please go away.* I
mentally pleaded,
squeezing my eyes shut as
tightly as they would go,
as though it would make
them go away. *Please just
leave me alone.*

Please.

Please.

Please...

I opened my eyes and
screamed.

Where am I?

A million thoughts rushed
through my head,

Not again...

I looked around at my
surroundings and cocked my
head in confusion.

*If I'm not in a forest
where the hell am I?*

My eyes adjusted to the
blackness and I rubbed my
eyes to check if it would
go away. I was sitting on
the floor in a heap, and I
dragged my cardigan back
over my shoulders as I
spun my head around to see
a doorway behind me. The
doorway was broken and
crooked, flaking wood
peeling of the dull green
paint. Above the doorway
was a cracked sign, with
bold letters faded with
time plastered across the
off-white background. I

140

stood up and the
floorboards creaked
underneath me, and dust
rose off the ground,
dancing around my toes, as
I walk gradually over to
the doors. I stood in
front of them and slammed
my palms on the handles,
pulling them back and
forth with great
difficulty as the doors
shuddered; I pulled them
as hard as I could as
though they would break
from their hinges. But it
didn't work. My hands
collapsed to the side and
I look at the debris
filled ground. During my
attempt to open the doors,
the sign had fallen of and
crumpled to the floor,
just in front of my bare

141

feet. I bent down warily
and picked up the sign,
carefully blowing the dust
and wiping the grime away
from the lettering with
the sleeve of my cardigan
dragged over my fist. I
stared at the sign for a
while until I realised
what it read.

L'HOTEL D'AMORE

What the-

Chapter Fourteen

"I am alive."

I squeezed my eyes shut
and whispered over and
over again to myself,
desperately trying to
bring myself back to
reality but it wasn't
working, I was trapped in
what seemed like an
abandoned hotel in the

middle of France. *France.*
How did I end up in
France? Asking myself
rhetorical questions came
to a halt once I realised
it was only panicking me
more. Taking in a deep
breath I stood straight,
opened my eyes, and turned
around to face the long,
daunting hallway in front
of me.

I began to slowly stalk
down the hallway,
shivering with every
chilling, old portrait I
saw hammered roughly on
the walls. Within around
ten minutes (I decided
mentally, as even though
there was an incredible
amount of clocks on the
walls along the hallway,

all were set on a
particular time and did no
longer move correctly) I
reached the end and stood
in front of yet another
door. Now, this is what
lead me to the big
question, rather than
what's in there; do *I go*
in there?

I slapped myself harshly
around the face, and a
small, timid voice uttered
something in my ears; *stop
being so pathetic, you're
here now, walk through
that door- it's your
destiny.*

Destiny.

*Now that sounds
interesting.*

I blinked viciously and
pulled up my shoulders,
shrugged on my cardigan
slipping down my spine and
thumped my hand onto the
handle, gripping it
tightly as I pushed down
and yanked it forward,
opening the doorway to a
world in which I wasn't
sure I was entering.

A harsh bright light
washed over me as I stood
charily in the doorway and
stared into the glimmering
shine, streaking across my
entire body and brushing
against my cheekbones as I
tilted my head back and
closed my eyes. The light
hammered against my skin
as I lifted my arms to my
side and extended them

outwards, welcoming the
light as though it
cleansed me.

Unexpectedly, I opened my
eyes and returned back to
reality.

Lying on the hospital bed
in my room, the TV
shrieked in my ears and I
rolled out of bed to turn
it off. Standing blindly
in front of my bed, I
shook my head and sighed
deeply. I couldn't decide
on whether my emotion was
relief or horror.

Nevertheless, I swung open
my own door and stepped
into the ward hallway and
sat down with the other
patients. And as I sat on
the sofa next to Kate I

turned and saw the short
white shadow man standing
next to me, the accomplice
of the dark one. He opened
his murky mouth and
whispered a snake-like
voice that slithered into
my ears like fog on a
Sunday morning;

You are alive.

~

Later that day, I sat in
the lounge with Ella and
another girl. The other
girl was the girl whom I
had first met on my first
day here, and she had told
me about Natasha's
accident. She sat opposite
me and I studied her
quietly; small, pretty
face, with a few freckles

scattered around her nose
and cheeks. Pale, soft
skin that glowed almost
the same colour as her
light blonde hair, hung
loosely into plaits,
dripping onto her ribcage.
Purple shirt also went by
the name of Harriet, and
she held a bubbly, sweet
personality, which I loved
her for.

"What do you think ___?"

"Oh, um, sorry?" I blushed
in realisation that we
were having a
conversation, and I was
only gazing at Harriet's
beauty rather than
listening.

"Like, about running
away?"

149

Ella was an escape artist, sliding in and out of windows like a young Houdini and scampering down the street as far as she could before she gets caught by the staff chasing breathlessly after her. I cleared my throat and rubbed my eyes. Looking down at my fingers, I saw black crusted in flakes on the bridge of my knuckles, and I remembered I just rubbed off the makeup I was wearing.

"I think about it," I began, and Ella nodded. I cleared my throat again; I began to think I was coming down with something,

"Me too,"

"I've tried many times,"
Harriet chirped in, and we
turned to her as she
blushed and continued,
"I've almost succeeded
too, but I was caught
before I could-"

"Same." Ella bounced in
and I squinted. Too many
voices were in this
conversation and I was
becoming increasingly
confused. As much as I
would love to leave this
place, I know I need to be
here, so running away I
feel would be pointless. I
shuffled in my seat as I
grew more and more
uncomfortable. Harriet
noticed my scuffling, and

151

I looked up timidly to see
her eyes on me,

"How are you Harrie?"

"Grand," She replied, "And
you?"

"Fabulous," I joked, and
felt my lips turn up
slightly into a smile.
Smiling suddenly reminded
me of Donnie, and I
remembered how much I
missed him. I sprung off
the coach and over to the
office, where I waiting
for a staff member to turn
and face me,

"Can I call someone
please?"

The staff member nodded
and I stalked over to the

phone, where I punched the
number into the phone and
ran outside by the fish
tank, where the phone sat
on a table, waiting for
the phone to ring.

"I'm sorry ___, there's no
answer."

My shoulders slumped and
my head automatically
bowed. I scuffed my shoes
on the carpet and buried
my hands in my back jean
pockets,

"Never mind," I looked up
at the staff member and
smiled, before slouching
over to the sofa and
collapsing next to
Harriet,

"What's up?"

"Donnie isn't answering and he hasn't called for a while," I replied, and gulped,

"He said he might have to go to an inpatient last week,"

"Do you think-"

"I think he's been sent off to a Psychiatric Unit too."

Harriet paused, "Shit."

Chapter Fifteen

"How are you holding up?"

"Yeah, I'm actually alright,"

"Fabulous,"

"I've made some friends,"

"That's great, I'm glad,"

"Yeah," Donnie replied down the phone, his voice echoing around a clinical

environment, noises
screeching through the
phone into my ears.

I was right. His long term
suffering from self-harm
and depression had caught
up to him too.

"Will I see you this
weekend?" There was a
slight pause, which shook
my entire body,

"Hopefully,"

"Awesome," I said, and
flicked my hair back from
my face,

"I'll see you soon then,"

"Sure,"

I cleared my throat and
prepared to hang up,

"Goodbye,"

"I love you,"

"Love you too." Pushing
the phone onto the
receiver, I stalked into
the classroom and flung
myself on the chair in
front of a laptop.

"____?"

My hair flicked against my
face as I whirled around
to see my therapist
positioned in the doorway.
I sighed and got up,
following him to the
upstairs lounge. Trailing
behind him, I look at the
doors to each room of the

157

narrow hallway, in which I have only been through a handful of times for therapy. Door signs and name tags were plastered on the outside of doors, making sure everyone knew who was in each room. I threw myself on the sofa and flicked my leg over the other, bouncing in my seat as my foot pulsated with its very own heartbeat, and cracking my knuckles as he sat down on a chair in front of me in silence.

He reached into the dull, leather brief case perched on the floor beside him, leaning against a chair leg, and slid out an A4 sheet of paper, with ink

printed on both sides. He
leant forward and held it
out in front of me. I
angled my head to the side
and my lips turned into a
frown. I reached out and
took the paper from him,
placing it lightly in my
lap and skimming my eyes
across the writing; it was
my report.

NAME: ___ ____ ____

DATE: SUNDAY 15TH
SEPTEMBER 2013

AGE: 16

DIAGNOSIS: SELF HARM/
SUICIDAL IDEATION/

DEPRESSION/ PANIC ATTACKS/
SOCIAL   ANXIETY

CURRENT RISK LEVEL: **HIGH**/
MEDIUM/ LOW

MENTAL STATE: Reported that
she was 'not good'. Reports of
cutting on her arm, her hand and
her leg. She is refusing to say
how she did this. We found sharp
items on her when she returned
from leave. She refuses to show
us the cuts she has made. She
has ongoing thoughts of suicide.
She denies thoughts of
absconsion. She is refusing
family therapy. She appears to be
irritated but finds it hard to talk
about these feelings. She is
possibly prone to perceiving other

people's attempts to care for her as being hostile or intrusive.

I bent down and slipped the sheet into the folder I had left in front of my feet. I leant back and avoided eye contact, purposely staring outside the window. Rain trickled against the glass, causing speckles of water to make prints on the window. The sound of rain falling on the glass and the ground filled the room with serenity. After a pause which seemed like an eternity, he finally spoke,

"There's something
interesting about you"

I snorted and shook my
head, the corners of my
lips turning upwards into
a half smile.

"I don't think I get what
you mean,"

"I mean," He cleared his
throat and folded one leg
over the other, "I mean
that-look at you- you
listen to this rock music,
and I mean, you have blue
hair-" He brushed one hand
through his thick head of
white hair and
gesticulated at me with
the same hand,

"I just think perhaps you want all attention on you,"

I cut him off with a sharp laughter.

He's patronising.

I stood up swiftly and straightened my neck, grazing one palm over the scars laced across it. I bowed my head in a hasty nod and turned to face the door, speaking to the man behind me as I walked over to the door,

"You've got me figured out all wrong,"

I reached out to the door handle and yanked it from my palms and stepped into

163

the hallway outside.
Breathing a huge sigh of
relief I shut my eyes as I
stood outside the door.
Trailing carefully behind
down the stairs back down,
I stepped into the hallway
and the door to the ward
slipped quietly shut
behind me, releasing a
breath of air as though it
were sighing, as it softly
slammed shut.

I stalked into my room,
flinging the sheet of
paper behind me, and it
fluttered to the floor
like a distraught
butterfly. I ninja rolled
into my bed slammed face
down into my pillow, my
eyes tightly shut and my
shoulders shuddering,

164

though it was an enormous
effort to get myself to
start crying. My therapy
session was not great,
though neither was my
entire day- he just put
the cherry on top of a
revolting sundae (pun
intended).

Chapter Sixteen

I laid in bed until I
could no longer mourn for
my awful day. Breathing
deeply and whispering
calming words, I sat
upright and rubbed my
eyes, clearing them of
black and tears and
sorrow. Reaching my hand
up to my ear, I clasped
the earphone and pulled
hard on it so it fell to
my side, music still
screeching quietly in the

background, mirroring the
voices uttering around me;
voices buried beneath
surfaces and invisible
places, hatching into
darkness and in the gloomy
void in which I resided.

Flicking the tears
dripping from my eyes like
rain with my sleeve, I
picked up the iPod laying
next to my right thigh on
the bed. Popping open the
case I punched in the code
and grunted as the code
failed and in frustration
I threw it across the
room, watching it bounce
from the wall to the
carpeted floor, laying in
a lump on the ground.

I rolled out of bed and
stood in front of the
mirror. I was wearing a
black, skin tight skirt
stuck above my knees, and
lacy tights flowing up my
legs. *A Nightmare Before
Christmas* shirt hung
loosely over my abdomen,
and a dull green military
jacket with a Metallica
badge sewn on the back was
draped over my shoulders
and fell just above the
bottom of my skirt. I felt
near naked, I have
literally never worn a
skirt in my life. A new
start is what it was meant
to symbolize, but all I
could see in the mirror
was fat and
unattractiveness.

And the black smudge.

I am the black smudge.

Deriving from the paint I
drew myself slowly out of
the bucket and splattered
against the wall in the
form of a smudge.

Snapping out of my zoning
out stage I walked out of
my room and into the ward
hallway. I haven't spoken
to Donnie in three days.
He hasn't called. He's not
good. Or busy. Or doesn't
care.

Stones laid like bones
near the ocean that were
the girls in the hallway.
Invisible amongst the
ocean creatures, I reached
out for a hand but no one

gave it to me. I sat on
the sofa deep in thought
and stared ahead at the
girls, swimming rapidly
about like fish.

El was still away, and the
present I bought for
Donnie resided in my room
for his birthday on
Friday. I sent him a card
today on Monday. I think
no amount of words can
describe how much he means
to me anyway. Just a
sentence I would say if I
had the guts and courage,

*Darling, please understand
that if you're cold I will
keep you warm.*

It doesn't make sense
anyway, no one seems to

understand my hyperbole
and over-use of metaphors.

But that's irrelevant.

What is relevant is right
now, living in the now.

Carpe Diem. Seize the day.
All of that. Though I
don't believe in it
entirely, for I myself
can't see a future. I
snapped out of my fading
vision and was immediately
living again, became
oblivious to my previous
thoughts and was
immediately snatched up
into the moment, where
girls were chattering
around me about whatever
girls talk about.

"What's that?" Soul sat
opposite me, and pointed
at my wrist. I hurriedly
pulled down my sleeve and
shrugged,

"nothing."

"Oh, come on."

I dragged up my sleeve and
turned my wrist to face
the patients opposite,

"It's a ribbon tattoo,"

"is it real?" El buzzed,

"No, it's temporary," I
laughed softly and pulled
down my sleeve again,

"It's meant to stop self-
harm,"

"is it working?"

"No," I uttered after a short pause, "But it might work for you."

"Oh?"

"Here, look," I grabbed the pen sticking out between the pages of my diary and gripped it in my hands as I ran over to Soul; sitting and waiting expectantly on the sofa. I took her wrist and gradually pulled up her sleeve, baring faint trickles of white and red scars laced across her veins, like a veil over her porcelain skin.

I cleared my throat and steadied the pen as I

plunged it softly onto her wrist, making patterns as it flowed across her skin; dancing like fairies around a bonfire, tickling her flesh and creating a masterpiece. I came to a halt and held the pen back, cocking my head to admire my work. Soul lifted her wrist to her eyes and the corners of her mouth twitched into a smile.

Being wary of smudging, she twisted her hand around to show the rest of the girls the artwork she bared on her wrist. A few lines joined together to match the ribbon tattoo I had, and shading brought it to life as it skipped

across the lines and body
of the small image
covering scars.

"There," I said, and stood
back, "now stay safe for
Christ's sake.

Chapter Seventeen

"She tried to set herself on fire."

I swallowed a hard lump in my throat and buried my head into Soul's shoulder as I stayed in our embrace. Beth walked past but I couldn't look at her, she was sobbing hysterically as she stumbled down the pitch black hallway with paramedics and staff. I let go of Soul and we sat on the couch together, and as my whole body shook, I squeezed a pillow tightly in my arms for some sort of comfort. It was dark and cold and I felt too alone, despite being surrounded by Soul.

"I know this is upsetting to you but-"

"How did she do it?" Soul cut off the staff member abruptly with a question that viciously slithered from between her lips. I could see the sweat dripping from the staff member's head as he was reaching out for some sort of answer from somewhere within his brain,

"She had a lighter."

"Oh Jesus," I muttered and covered my face in my palms.

I wasn't only upset because of the distressed and dangerous state that Beth was in.

The black shadow man stood tall in the opposite side of the room, glowering at me with hollow eyes and scowling with a distasteful grin. His accomplice, White, stood by his side, like a child holding his mother's hand, or a young couple in love; though this love story was worse than Bonnie and Clyde, for harm and suicide was their ultimate goal for myself.

My panic attack commenced
and I revolved into
another world.

The forest was a second
home; dark and
unwelcoming, but familiar.
I don't feel safe there,
but then again, I don't
feel safe anywhere- except
from by Ella and Soul's
side. In this forest I was
no longer the black
smudge, I was more
important; the protagonist
of the story, the hero in
the film, the brave and
courageous leader. There,
I am more important than I
have ever been. Leading a
life as someone invisible-
even someone who dressed
boldly with gothic flare
and bright blue hair- I am

ignored by everyone, and
left, abandoned, by
everyone I have ever
become attached with.

Abandoned, rubbed away,
cleaned off and forgotten.

Though in the forest, the
dark, murky abyss that was
my alternate universe, I
was alone, again, though I
was allowed to march the
story along. And I could
too.

Walking around in the
forest, the tall shadow
man and his white
accomplice were my slaves.
They did what I wanted
them to do, rather than
the other way round. I
couldn't slice up my arms
or my neck, or strangle

myself in this world. They
couldn't make me if they
tried. This is my world.
Mine.

Beth screamed and I landed
like a rocket to earth
back into reality

Chapter Eighteen

Natasha screamed and I jumped back. My arms were drenched and my short sleeves were soaked with shower water and flower smelling shampoo. I scrubbed at her head in a circular motion with my palms, but did so hastily, for the door was gradually closing. When Natasha asked me to wash her hair for her I underestimated the difficulty, though I was too afraid to get caught for patients are not allowed in each other's rooms. I plunged

my fingertips into the
conditioner bottle and
smothered the soapy
substance all over her
long, hanging hair, tipped
over the bath and under
the running shower. Water
splashed everywhere as I
began to scrub it off,
running onto the floor and
bumping carelessly into
towels. She was squealing
and I was giggling
hysterically, as I
attempted to wash her hair
as quickly as I could
under the boiling hot
water spraying all over me
and the walls,

"Done," I said quickly,
and flicked the water off
my hands, inspecting my
drenched sleeve. I began

to sprint towards the door
to her room, wedged open
with my coat, "I'm
literally going to run out
now because-"

A staff member stood
solemnly in the doorway.

"Fuck." Natasha breathed,

"Out." The staff member
copied,

"Right," I hurriedly
picked up the jacket
strewn on the floor, "I'm
going, sorry,"

I ran out the door and the
staff member waltzed into
Natasha's room, as I ran
into mine preparing myself
for a lecture on what I
did wrong.

I reminisced on how dreadful the night before was. We had spent the evening, Soul and Natasha and I, sprawled nervously in the lounge playing Guitar Hero, though even a challenging game based on rock music that we all enjoyed so much, could not cure the evening no matter what. We refused to go in our rooms, for we knew we would not be safe. And I was here to be safe. And I would try my absolute hardest to stay strong. I swallowed two sleeping tablets, and after about twenty minutes, I began to grow tired. I glanced at the clock, but it was only a blur; a bundle of

numbers and pulsating
white-ness.

1 am.

I crawled into my room.

Half an hour flew past,
and I laid jaded in my
bed, curled under the
duvet and shaking
vigorously with anxiety.
No one had come to check
on me. I was on fifteen
minute checks. I flipped
out of bed into the
darkness of my room, and
sprinted back out of the
door into the ward
hallway. Ella and Soul
were lounged on the
sofa's, twiddling their
fingers. Ella turned to
look at me as I spoke,

"No one's checked on me."

"Oh?" Soul replied, and
looked up from her
crossword puzzle. I nodded
my head, and dragged my
knees up onto the sofa,
coiling my arms around
them and burrowing my chin
in the bridge between both
knees. A staff member
walked over and stood in
the gap betwixt both
sofas, hands on her waist
stood in an authoritative
stance,

"Bedtime guys, come on,"

"No," Soul muttered, and I
shook my head,

"Why?"

187

"I'm not going in my
room," Soul uttered, and
flicked a strand of
brunette hair from her
face,

"I don't feel save in my
room," I murmured, and the
staff member turned to
face me,

"Why honey? Wanna talk
about it?" I shook my head
and she sighed,

"She's good to talk to,"
Ella said, "You might as
well." I nodded and stood
up, tugging on my pyjama
shirt drooping massively
over my body. I stalked
into my room and the staff
member followed, as I
flung myself onto the bed
and curled into an upright

188

foetal position, burying
my forehead in my palm.

"What's going on honey?"

"*Everything*," I muttered,
and shut my eyes tightly,
as though it could make
the pain go away. The tall
shadow man stood next to
my door without his
accomplice this time, and
he stood towering over the
staff member and I,
constantly whispering.
Constantly.

"It might help if you
talk,"

"I want to do
something...bad."

"Like what sweetie?"

I was silent. I couldn't
give away what I wanted to
do. I couldn't. Shaking my
head and continued to keep
my eyes closed.

"Come on honey. It's a
journey, and I know it's
hard, but I also know that
you can do it," she placed
her had onto my shoulder
and I felt her eyes on me,
"you can do it, I believe
that you can finish this
journey."

I swallowed harshly and
released my hand from my
forehead, but continued to
look down,

"Give it to me honey,"
slowly, and unsurely, I
turned towards my bedside
table and picked up the

alarm clock waiting
expectantly on top of it.
Underneath was one half of
a bobby pin, with blood
and skin stuck to one
side. I picked it up, and
gave it to the staff
member, avoiding any eye
contact.

"Thank you," She gripped
it in her fist, "is there
anything else?"

I nodded,

"What is it?"

"Something you can't take
away."

"Such as?"

"The bath tub." She nodded
and walked out of the

room, leaving me to curl
back into a ball. A minute
or two passed and she
waltzed back in with a set
of keys in her hand. And a
door stopper. She wedged
open my door and walked
over to my bathroom.

"I'm going to lock it,
ok?"

I muttered a response and
she nodded, pushing the
key into the lock and
twisting it shut.

"I'm here if you need to
talk honey, ok?"

"Ok," I whispered
hoarsely, and she walked
out. I sat there for a
while, cuts stinging,
tears welling up in my

eyes and the lights
flickering dauntingly on
and off. After about ten
minutes of sitting in a
ball sobbing quietly, and
reached for the switch
behind the table and
switched off the light,
twisting into bed and
drawing the duvet over my
head, falling into a
somewhat peaceful sleep.

Chapter Nineteen

Gripping the safety
scissors in my fingers I
perched on the edge of the
sofa and buried my feet
underneath the body of
Soul, sitting cross legged
in front of me,

"Are you sure about this?"

"Yes,"

"Do you trust me?"

"Yes," She giggled and I
brushed the hair across
her face, reaching from
the back to the front. I
took in a deep breath and

began to snip in layers,
feathering the hair across
her face as I chopped her
brunette locks. Hair
trickled to the floor and
over my legs as I
carefully trimmed a fringe
into her hair, and I
kicked it away softly with
my sock. I sat back and
dropped the scissors to
the floor, admiring my
work,

"Done,"

"Oh my god,"

"Soul, it looks fucking
awesome."

"You look so nice,"
Natasha breathed, and
clasped her hands to her
mouth,

195

"Thanks," Soul beamed.

~

Standing wearily outside
the doorway to Samantha's
room, I waited expectantly
for her to notice. She
spun around and motioned
towards me, long fingers
beckoning for me to enter
her room,

"___! Come here,"

I stepped into her room,
and a warm aroma hit me
like a puff of smoke. She
reached carefully for my
hand, shaking vigorously
as she did so,

"My hands are shaking,
sorry,"

"It's ok honey,"

"Thank you-" She dragged
up my sleeve and pushed a
large, beaded bracelet
onto my wrist, "-for the
letter, I'll miss you,"

"I-I'll miss you too," I
choked on my words, overly
surprised at the very kind
gesture Samantha had just
given me. And only because
I wrote her a leaving
letter for she was leaving
that day, being
transferred to another
hospital, for her fragile
body could no longer be
kept here. I reached out
my arms and wrapped them
carefully around her, and
we stood in an embrace

until it was time for her
to say goodbye.

That evening, we walked
down to the dinner table
and munched on crumbs with
sorrow. Natasha, Harriet,
Ella, Soul and I were
taken upstairs with a
member of staff after
dinner had finished, and
as we opened the door of
the dining room and
stepped into the hallway
of the hospital, we
crossed paths with a door.
This door wasn't any door;
it was *the* door. The one
you left to go home, the
one you came through to
get here, the all holy,
almighty door, that held
the key to absconstion if
it were to be left open.

Natasha skulked down the
hallway, and I trailed
behind her, as we chatted
about something or other.
She flung herself to the
door and I stood
expectantly behind her,
gazing at the lock clasped
next to the door, which
could only be opened with
a fob key. She threw her
fists on the door and I
waited to her the clicking
noise, meaning the door
could not be opened but
suddenly-

Oh shit.

Natasha gasped and
sprinted out of the opened
door which ticked open
with ease once she banged
it slightly, and Ella spun

around. Noticing the door
was open, she screamed,
and sprinted after
Natasha. The staff member
cried out,

"STAY HERE," and flailed
her hands towards us.

She dashed out of the open
door, after the girls
galloping away into the
distance, like escapee
horses riding into the
sunset; a better place. I
stood in the open doorway
and stuck my foot outside,
ready to sprint, ready to
run away from all of this;
I contemplated until I
could contemplate no
longer. Eventually, in
this miniscule second
stretched out like a small

tablecloth over a large
table, I picked my foot up
and placed it behind the
doorway, back into the
hospital. We ran towards
the dining room and
Harriet burst through the
doors,

"E-Ella and Natasha," she
gulped harshly and
motioned outside, "they
ran away."

Sitting on the windowsill
of the lounge windows, we
looked out eagerly,
waiting in expectation to
see Ella's pink hair or
Natasha's wavy locks
appear from around the
corner to the hospital.

"Where are they headed?" I
questioned softly, aiming

my question generally at the girls as we all continued to gaze expectantly out of the looking glass. There was a silence that overwhelmed the room with emptiness. Without looking at me, Harriet spoke into the window,

"The train tracks," she said,

"Ella would jump."

At that exact moment, we heard the noise of a train, and the horn hooting as it wafted past, leaving a ghostly presence in the lounge. We spun around and lock our sight on each other. I gasped and tears rippled down my

202

face. I walked over to
Harriet and threw my arms
around her, feeling her
watery cheeks brush
against my shoulder. Soul
leant her head against
mine as I stood in our
squeeze.

Silence bared it's hollow
soul.

I let go of Harriet and
Soul and swept the tears
from my face. We looked
back out the window and
breathed heavily, tears
dripping down our faces as
we muttered silent prayers
that they would both be ok
and that they would come
back.

A police car emerged from
around the corner and I
sighed drastically.

*Please tell me they're in
there.*

We clambered against the
window and raised our
shoulders, sitting in the
silent tension as we saw
the door of the police car
open. Pink hair clambered
out of the vehicle,

"ELLA!"

"Oh thank fuck," I cried
and flickered my eyes to
Harriet, who was still
muttering quietly but had
stopped crying. She was
refusing to go back into
the hospital, and two
police officers dragged

her through she holy door
by her arms which were
clasped by her side,
gripping onto the arms of
the police officers as she
tried to push them away,
but to no avail. We
sprinted out of the lounge
and stood by the entrance
of the ward, shaking and
sniffling as we waited for
Ella to appear. The door
swung open and Ella was
pushed in by the Police,
Natasha following swiftly
behind. Harriet and Soul
and I sobbed and I jumped
into Ella's arms,
squeezing her tightly as
though I could never let
go, and I never would.

"I was so worried about
you," I whispered into her

ear as I let go and
grasped onto her biceps,

"We were so scared, I'm *so
glad* that you're ok." She
nodded, and I released my
grip as she went to hug
Harriet. I slung my arms
around Natasha,

"Never do that to me
again," I whimpered, and
tears slithered down my
cheeks again, as she
squeezed me tightly and
cried softly into my hair.

"It's over now," I
muttered, and swayed her
softly, "It's gonna be
ok."

Chapter Twenty

Slipping into the pearly abyss, I shut my eyes and wished for a safe landing.

Falling down the rabbit hole was not as great as Alice had made it out to be.

My hand throbbed as I remembered in painful realisation of how hard I had beaten up the wall earlier on, and I gripped it tightly as I flew down and down, twirling and flipping into the shadowy gulf. I landed in a crumpled heap on the ground and found myself in wonderland. Oh, my wonderful wonderland, my murky trees and burning aroma; my very own dimension. My very own secret hide away. Mine, all mine. And like cheap whisky, it is always there. Until I am called back of course. I walked around slightly, circling around the leaves and weaving in and out of the flaking trees, peeling as though they were burnt and falling into the darkness. I walked around my world, breathing in the smoky scent and shivering against the cold night breeze. My path lit meekly by the moon, I turned a corner and ended up in

where I began. Again and
again. The infinite abyss.

No, no...

My trees began to fade and
the forest floor full of
leaves began to
disintegrate and crumble
away, as I rapidly scooped
up the leaves in my palms
I tried fixing them back
together as they fell to
the ground like ash.
Chimes echoed in the
distance and I heard a
loud and reeling telephone
ringing. I opened my eyes
and I was back in the ward
hallway, standing
obliviously in the middle
of the room. I heard quiet
muttering until my name
began to ring in my ears,

"_____?_____?"

"Uh, yes, sorry,"

"Phone call,"

"Ok," I stumbled over to
the phone and collapsed
onto the floor, slinging
the phone by my ear like a
gun flung over my
shoulder. There are a
dozen reasons in this gun.

"Hey you,"

"Hey," I whispered back
and closed my eyes.
Donnie.

"How are you doing?"

"Uhm," I replied, and
shifted the phone by my

211

earlobe, "really really
really, not good."

"Oh, honey..."

"How are you?"

"Oh come on," He moaned,"
I am just *grand*."

I shook my head and
muttered a half hearted
reply,

"How I am is irrelevant,"

"No, no its not-"

"Why aren't you ok?"

I sighed and brushed a
strand of hair behind my
ear.

"It's been a horrible day
and-" I swallowed a hard

lump in my throat and willed myself to not sob,"-and I don't think I can do it anymore."

Tears trickled like a waterfall across my cheek, and I whispered delicately into the phone, "and I just want to-" I choked on my words and broke into hysterics.

"___, you can do this," Donnie spoke softly and carefully, picking his words, "I love you, and I believe in you, you're stronger than you lead yourself to believe."

"I can't-"

"*You can't leave me now.*"

I laughed quietly and answered abruptly, wiping the tears from under my eyes, "You can't say that,"

"Oh but I can," He whispered, and I felt him take a sharp intake of breath," I *need* you, ___."

I inhaled steadily and cleared my throat.

"Just, please stay safe tonight,"

"I'll try if you do too,"

"Promise?"

"Promise."

"I love you,"

"Likewise."

Chapter 21

This isn't fair, don't you try to bring this on me

My love for you was bulletproof but you're the one who shot me.

Sitting with Soul on the couch I sung in my head, and as the echoes reverberated against my skull I contemplated the relevance of the lyrics to my life. *But you're the one who shot me.* The cleaning ladies rolled past with their trolley topped with cleaning potions and paper towels, walking in and out of rooms with whimsicality. I snapped out of my oblivious daydream as Soul muttered something in my

ear. I jumped out of my
skin and threw it on the
floor, stamping on it
multiple times as I heard
what Soul whispered. My
eyes widened and I felt
tears well up in my brain.
I shut my eyes and
squeezed them tightly,
willing Soul to be joking
or lying and bluffing or
anything but honest.

She stood up.

*Soul don't fucking do
this.*

She walked around on the
spot for a while and I
thought she'd forgotten
about what she said she
would do. She clasped her
hand over her mouth and
stared blankly into the

distance, eyes dead and
legs holding up her body
limply, as she flung her
hand around by her side
limply, as she flung her
hand around her side with
every uncertain step. She
turned and faced the
hallway.

What is she looking at?

She began to walk down the
hallway and I expected she
would go to her room,
unsafe and vulnerable by
herself. My gaze followed
her down the hallway and
past the cleaning trolley.
She suddenly began to
sprint.

I launched myself off the
sofa and hurled my body
towards her, chasing her

down the hallway and
burning my bare feet on
the carpeted floor. I
tackled her to the ground
before she opened the door
to her room and gripped
onto what she held in her
hand, wriggling it free
from her tight grip and
uttering loudly in her
ear, "give it to me, Soul,
give it-"

"NO! No, please-"

"*SOUL!*"

"*I WANT TO DIE.*"

"*FUCKING GIVE IT TO ME-*" I
pulled it from her palms
and fell backwards as she
fell into my arms and
sobbed, crying
hysterically and curling

219

her arms around me. A
staff member peeled her
arms from me as they
walked into her room with
her and did not come out
for the rest of the day.

I sat on the sofa again
and shut my eyes. I
mentally cursed at myself;
she told me, why didn't I
go after her sooner, why
didn't I say something,
why am I so pathetic.

I looked down at the
object in my hands and her
voice saying what she said
ricocheted in my brain
again.

*"I want to drink that
bleach."*

Chapter 22

Lockdown.

Someone smashed a jam jar.

What the actual fuck.

The kitchen was locked for the remainder of the entire day, for plates and various jars were being misused. Dealing sharp objects was described as sick by myself, though whilst I was asleep, this was in fact occurring. Everyone's room was to be searched and I made it clear to a member of staff on how uncomfortable I was about people going through my things,

"Well if you have nothing to hide then you won't worry about it!"

"Chelsea that's not the
fucking point-"

"language-"

"I just don't want people
going through my shit!"

"LANGUAGE-"

"they're going to mess it
all up,"

"well-"

"for fucks sake Chelsea,"

"oh forget it."

Staff were following
around particular girls
like lost puppies, and I
hid in the classroom
dreading my room search.

Soon enough, a staff
member came to me,

"come outside please,"

I shakily got up from my
chair and followed the
staff member to my room.
Staff where clustered
around my bedroom with
rubber gloves on, picking
the badges off my coat
with lack of delicacy.

"We're taking away these
DVDs," I looked into the
box they thrust in front
of my eyes and I glared
at the cases shoved
inside. Two 18 rated
movies were thrown in
and I shrugged it off.

*I'm not eighteen so I
can't argue with that.*

Two fifteen rated films
were also thrown in and
I pointed my finger at
them,

"I'm sixteen and these
are for my film
studies,"

"They're not
appropriate-"

"I need them,"

She sighed drastically
and rubbed her temples,

"Ok ok," She picked them
up and forced them in my
palms,

"thank you."

She waved of my reply
and I placed the two
films back where they
were before stalking out
of my room and making my
way back to the
classroom.

~

"_____?!"

I yanked the earphones
out of my ear and sat up
attentively.

"_____?!" I twirl my
feet so they were
hanging off the bed and
jumped off, rolling
smoothly onto the

carpeted floor and
standing up again,
gliding to the door. I
walked through and stood
obliviously in the
middle of the hallway,
turning frantically
around to see who was
calling my name,

"___, there you are,"

I nodded swiftly and
brushed a strand of hair
from my eyes,

"phone call."

I skipped to the table
in which the handset sat
waiting expectantly for
me to pick up the phone.

it rang and I picked up
on the second sound,

"hello?"

"Hi you," I laughed half
heartedly, expecting my
parents to be on the
other line,

"Hey Donnie,"

"How are you?"

"Oh I'm grand," I tucked
a strip of blue behind
my ear and rubbed
mascara from my eye,
"Seeing you in two
days,"

"yeah, about that-"

"what did you do."

He cleared his throat
and I pictured him
closing his eyes,
thinking of some
plausible way of
explaining himself,

"These girls broke a
fuse box to open all the
doors,"

"you didn't..."

"I ran away with them."

"Oh Donnie..."

"We had a plan,"

"I suspect it wasn't a
good nor safe plan,"

"It was a bad plan."

"so I can't-"

"I'm not allowed home,"

"I'm not surprised," I
pressed my palm to my
forehead and shut my
eyes as though they were
sighing, "just, don't
make any more stupid
plans with your new
friends, ok?"

"yes ma'am,"

"I'm serious,"

"I promise I won't," he
breathed deeply and
sighed, "I miss you too
much."

"I miss you too,"

"stay safe, ok?"

"I'll try."

Chapter 23

Sitting in a corner in my wardrobe, Soul banged against the door, begging for me to open it. I choked on my words as I couldn't breathe, and I curled up further, pulling tighter on the cable wrapped tightly around my neck. Soul fell against the door and it slipped open as she stormed in and threw herself in front of me on the floor,

"Let go," she gripped the cable but I refused to budge, squeezing tightly with white knuckles as I pulled harder, feeling the blood fill my eyes, "please *let go*."

She pulled and it began to
slip free,

"no," I screamed, "no!" I
gurgled my words against
the barricade on my
throat, but as Soul pulled
harder I released my grip
and she unwrapped the
cable as it slithered to
the floor like a python.

I was dragged up from the
floor by Natasha, Soul and
a staff member, and was
hurled onto the hallway
couch, curled into Soul's
arms as she rocked me back
and forth,

"why did you do that for?"

"I-" I swallowed harshly
and closed my eyes,
feeling Soul's breath

233

against my cheek, "I just
want to die."

"I know, trust me, I
know," she leant in closer
and closed her eyes too,
"But I'm worried about
you, please don't do that
again,"

"I love you dude,"

"I love you too,"

I sat in her arms until I
felt tired enough to fall
asleep.

Chapter 24

Do you ever get that
moment, that false
security of true
realisation. An epiphany
of what has truly
happened. When you stop,
and the whole world stops
with you, and in that
moment, you swear that you
figure out the meaning of
your life. The one moment
where you pause and think;
*how did I make it this
far?* You think, I've made
it this far, why stop now?
Then, I can't go on. So
many thoughts travelling
at the speed of light,
rushing in and out of your
flickering brain cells,
tricking your imagination,
making you believe what
you want to believe, and

forcing a false reality on
yourself.

Have you ever gotten that
moment, where you wish you
were never even born at
all?

Well, even if you can't go
on; you'll go on. And even
if you don't want to;
you'll end up wanting to.
Your brain is dead, a
thick skull filled with
emptiness, but the trick
is, you can fill it up
with whatever you want.
Fill it with passion,
creativity, love. Fill it
with colour and
imagination, memories and
music. Fill it with dreams
and serenity and
happiness. Pick people's

brain's and cram your own
with whatever you want to;
fill it to the brim with
laughter and life.

You *can* get through this.
Your own struggles are
irrelevant; just pause and
take that moment, grasp it
and embrace it with open
arms, squeeze it and never
let go. Hold onto that
moment, and breathe.

You can last forever with
the Pandora's box in your
mind.

You are infinite.

Chapter 25

I woke up startled.

"I am alive" I uttered
with my eyes still shut.
What is waiting for me
when I open my eyes? My
room at the hospital, my
room at home, or a forest
or an abandoned hotel?

What's waiting for me?

I opened my eyes.

Monitors beeped around me
and scalpels hung loosely
from the tray by my bed.
My eyes flickered down to
my body; a hospital gown
was shawled over my person
and I was coiled in a thin
crotched blanket. The bed
was rickety and
uncomfortable, and a
curtain was drawn around

the small area around my
bed, a dusty blue curtain
that hid me from the other
patients. I heard
footsteps occurring from
outside the curtain and I
brushed the hair quickly
back from my face. As I
dropped my hand I noticed
a thin needle plunged into
the vein in my hand,
connection to a wire that
sunk into a bag hung from
a pole by my bed. I sat
up, moving my drip
slightly, and attempted to
listen to the voices now
commencing from behind the
curtain.

The voices sounded like a
man and a woman, the woman
being a doctor and the man

being a nurse of some
sort.

"Are you going to tell
them?"

"It's not good news, I'd
rather not-"

"Oh you don't say," the
man interrupted, "It's not
my place to talk with the
parents,"

"well I'm making it your
place,"

"look, check on her first
then we'll decide,"

"She's not going to just
spontaneously wake up-"

"*check.*"

The curtain was slowly
pulled back and a middle
aged man and a young,
pretty woman in her
twenties stood in front of
me, jaws dropped to their
chest. I wriggled
uncomfortably in my bed
and swiped a strand of
hair behind my ear,

"Hi," I cooed, as the
monitor beeped along with
the rhythmic knocking of
my heart,

"You're...awake,"

"I am indeed,"

"Good afternoon,"

I tipped my head in reply
and the woman straightened
her skin tight skirt and

243

cleared her throat, as the man still stood there with an expression that seemed like he was overly pleased with himself,

"Excuse us a second," the woman squeaked and twirled around, dragging the man outside the curtain and slamming the door shut behind them. I suppressed a laugh and nodded my head towards the other side of the curtain. I leant closer to the side and realised I could hear a sort of rustling and clicking of tapping into a mobile phone.

Someone is next to me.

I threw off my blanket and spun my feet off the bed,

landing delicately on the floor. I turned to my drip and grabbed it by its pole. I began to drag it behind me as I walked over to the other side of the curtain. Slowly and steadily, I began to draw the material back, allowing light to burst through the windows and through the gap which appeared from behind the curtains.

There, sat a shadowed person, lounged on the hospital bed next to mine, just behind the curtain. I walked wearily over, pulling my drip behind me, engulfed by the sun.

I cleared my throat to get their attention, and sure enough, they turned their head.

I gasped.

"What are you doing here?"

"The same reason you're here,"

"why am I here?"

"You can't remember?"

"I remember being in a mental hospital but that's all,"

"you were never in a mental hospital, only this one,"

"what? I-"

"We jumped in front of a
train Angela,"

"Is that my name?"

"Yeah,"

I grasped my hair in my
hands and burrowed my face
in my palms.

What the fuck is going on.

"Donnie,"

"yes?"

"I'm scared,"

"I'm here now, don't be
scared," he sat up
slightly and smiled, light
glowing around him like an
aura, like we died and
were in heaven.

"What happened?"

"We jumped in front of a
train together but it
stopped before it hit us.
You've been in a coma for
two months."

"And in the two months I
haven't been in a mental
hospital?"

"No, you've been asleep,"

"I've been asleep," I
looked up and tears
slithered down my face,
"I've been asleep,"

Donnie twirled around and
stood up, walking slowly
over to me, he bent down
and wrapped his arms
around me,

"You're back now, it's
ok,"

"So, Soul? Natasha? Ella?
They're not real?"

"Soul?"

I swallowed a hard lump in
my throat and more tears
dribbled down my face like
a complex river, "tall,
skinny brunette?"

"Emma?"

He readjusted the collar
around his neck and
focused his gaze to the
floor. He gulped harshly.
He raised his head and
looked me dead in the
eyes; baring eyes like a
corpse and an
expressionless face.

"She's dead."

His sentence hit me like a bomb; two awful words that left a sour taste in my mouth, and a burning sensation on the back of my neck. An unexpected kill that left me breathless, Soul had been my best friend throughout this hazy daydream, and now she is gone without me meeting her in real life? I felt lightheaded and dizzy and I stumbled backwards, falling into bed spine first, hitting it harshly like the two words that slipped into my ears like daggers.

She's dead.

Dead.

Donnie continued to speak
but I blocked out his
words, allowing one or two
phrases to enter my brain
as I attempted to process
the sudden bombshell.

"Natasha's called Tash I
guess. And Ella? I think
you mean Bella... Pink
hair?"

I nodded and slapped my
hand against my forehead
and buried my face in my
palms.

"what happened to them?"

*Tell me they didn't die
too.*

"they were on the train
that stopped for us," he
stroked the back of my

251

head and tucked a flick of hair behind my ear, "nice girls,"

"yeah," I muttered and burrowed my head in his shoulder, "this is all too much,"

"It's over now," he kissed me delicately on the cheek," it's all over."

I looked up and steadied myself, trying to pull myself up with my shoulder, forcing my hands next to me on the bed and hauling my body off the bed. I focused my gaze on Donnie's, attempting to figure him out, guess what he was thinking, guess what he would say next. But no to avail; my questions had found their answers- Soul, or should I say Emma, is dead, and this whole entire time has been a lie. I almost died and landed myself in a coma, while Donnie bailed on the jump at the last minute and landed himself to safety. I can't blame him though, he did the right thing, not jumping, look where I ended up.

"are we going to a mental hospital?"

"let's focus on getting you out of this one first,"

I bit my bottom lip and shut my eyes, "I just want heaven to help us."

He laughed, and for that
moment, I could picture
what he filled his brain
with; love, life, passion.
I envied his brain and
longed for the day where I
could fill my own. In that
second; I thought of my
family. How much I missed
them, and how much I
wanted to go home.

My hollow skull suddenly
burned. It whirred and
clicked and I felt it
absorb like a sponge.

It was filled with my
first emotion, my first
filling; love.

"One day," He stroked my
chin with his forefinger
and thumb, "I love you
Angela,"

I swallowed the hard lump
in my throat and felt my
brain smile. I grinned
like the Cheshire cat
clock, I swum into the
open like the underwater
ward, and I saw the black
shadow man and his
accomplice in the corner
of my eyes. They smiled,
and gave me their
blessing, standing over me
like my new guardian
angels. Soul was gone, but
she would live in my heart
forever.

I turned up to corners of
my mouth and widened my
eyes as they glistened
with hope, embracing the
sun, before I opened my
lips to speak,

"Likewise."